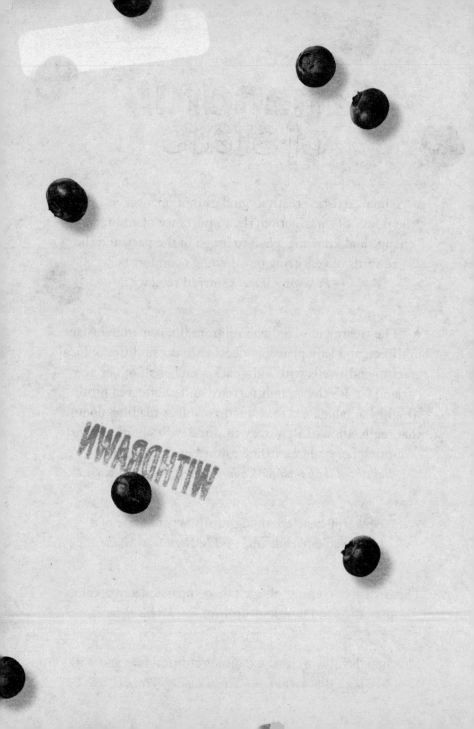

CYNTHIA LORD

a handful of stars

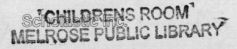

Copyright © 2015 by Cynthia Lord

This book was originally published in hardcover by Scholastic Press in 2015.

All rights reserved. Published by Scholastic Inc., *Publishers since 1920*. SCHOLASTIC and associated logos are trademarks and/or registered trademarks of Scholastic Inc.

The publisher does not have any control over and does not assume any responsibility for author or third-party websites or their content.

No part of this publication may be reproduced, stored in a retrieval system, or transmitted in any form or by any means, electronic, mechanical, photocopying, recording, or otherwise, without written permission of the publisher. For information regarding permission, write to Scholastic Inc., Attention: Permissions Department, 557 Broadway, New York, NY 10012.

This book is a work of fiction. Names, characters, places, and incidents are either the product of the author's imagination or are used fictitiously, and any resemblance to actual persons, living or dead, business establishments, events, or locales is entirely coincidental.

ISBN 978-0-545-70028-3

10 9 8 7 6 5 4 3   17 18 19 20 21

Printed in the U.S.A.   40
First printing 2017

Book design by Nina Goffi

To Island Readers and
Writers and to all the
children they serve

Chapter 1

The only reason I ever spoke to Salma Santiago was because my dog ate her lunch.

Sometimes life is like a long road leading from one "if" to another. If Lucky hadn't slipped out of his collar, I wouldn't have been running across the blueberry barrens in late July, yelling, "Lucky! No! Come! Treats!" trying every phrase that dog knew, praying one of them would slow him down long enough for me to grab him.

"Leash! Bacon! Go for a ride? Cheese!" But for a blind, old, black Labrador retriever, Lucky's really fast.

Especially on those wide-open barrens where there's nothing to bump into and every which way to go.

Wild Maine blueberry bushes grow less than a foot high, but they're thick and pokey. My ankles were scraped up and stinging as I sprinted past another WINTHROP BLUEBERRIES. NO TRESPASSING sign.

On Sundays, I always see Mr. Winthrop at church, dressed up and sitting in his family's pew. I hoped he'd remember the whole "Forgive those who trespass against us" part of the Lord's Prayer if he saw me. I was praying, too, but with my eyes open, afraid if I closed them, Lucky would be gone.

Please stop Lucky. Please stop him. No, not the road! I begged, terrified Lucky would get hit by that big Winthrop truck coming, carrying tall rainbow stacks of plastic bins of blueberries.

Brakes squealed. "Hey!" the driver of the truck shouted at me. "Get off those bushes!"

"It's my dog!" I yelled.

If that driver hadn't slammed on his brakes, and if we hadn't yelled at each other, the girl might not have noticed me running after Lucky. I saw her from the corner of my eye: a flash of long black ponytail and orange T-shirt leaping over the strings that marked off the blueberry fields into lanes for raking. She ran as fast as a gale wind across those barrens, dropping her blueberry rake and grabbing a backpack off a pile. As she got closer to Lucky, she pulled a sandwich and a little bag of chips out of her backpack.

Lucky wasn't listening to "come" or any of his favorite words, but the crinkle of that chip bag pulled his ears right back.

If she hadn't given him her lunch, Lucky would probably still be running across Maine—maybe all the way into Canada by now.

When I caught up, I was so out of breath that I couldn't even speak. All I could do was nod at the girl giving Lucky her sandwich. She looked about twelve years old, same as me. Her hair was wispy around her face where it was coming loose from her ponytail and she had a smear of dirt on her cheek. Even so, she was pretty. She was probably from one of the migrant families that drive here for a few weeks every summer. They come in old trucks, campers, and cars from Mexico and Florida and other far-off places to rake the blueberries that grow wild in the barrens. I don't usually talk to those kids and they don't usually talk to me. They don't stay here long enough for us to be friends.

As Lucky licked peanut butter from his mouth, I wrapped the collar around his neck—a tighter fit this time. By the time I had it buckled and the leash clipped on, the girl was walking back to her blueberry lane.

"Thanks!" I yelled. "And sorry about your lunch. I didn't mean to let him eat your whole sandwich!"

But I guess no one would want a half-eaten-by-a-dog sandwich anyway.

Surrounded by people in other lanes, she swept the bushes with her aluminum blueberry rake. A blueberry rake looks like a metal dustpan with teeth. The back end is an open box with a handle or two on top. The front end has a row of sharp tines. You push the tines through the low-growing bushes and then tip the rake up and back so the berries are scooped off and roll down to collect in the back. It's hard, tiring work. A man near the girl yelled something in Spanish and she laughed. She didn't look up, though. Just kept scooping and tipping.

Walking home, I scolded Lucky, but he didn't seem one teeny bit sorry for all the trouble he'd caused.

Maybe because he got a sandwich out of it.

Or maybe because it felt so good to run wild again; full-tilt across those wide-open barrens the way a blind dog barely ever gets to run anymore.

Or maybe because Lucky can sense things people can't. Dr. Katz, our veterinarian, says that when a dog loses his sight, the other senses get sharper to make up for it. She may be right, because Lucky sure heard that chip bag and smelled that peanut butter.

But I think it's more than that.

If Lucky hadn't led me over those blueberry barrens, we might never have met that girl, Salma Santiago. And I think Lucky knew that we needed her, maybe even more than she needed us.

Chapter 2

"I've raised you better than that," my grandmother said that night when I told her how Lucky ate a girl's sandwich and chips. "Lily, you're going to bring that child something else to eat, in case that was all she had."

"But Mémère, it happened at lunchtime," I said. "She'll think it's weird if I show up with food *now*. And how am I going to find her? I don't even know her name!"

"Pépère will take you over to their camp."

My grandfather opened his mouth, like he was going to protest. Then he shut it. Pépère likes to say that when

Mémère gets an idea in her head, she's like a hurricane and everybody else should dive for cover.

"Mrs. Lamont brought in some frozen *tourtière* for the store this morning," Mémère said. "I still have a couple to sell. You'll bring that child's family one of those."

"You want me to bring a pork pie? To the camp? But I don't even know if she likes tourtière!" I said. "Maybe she's a vegetarian."

Mémère tipped her head down to look at me over her eyeglasses. "I'll get you a sturdy bag. Those pies are heavy."

"If I bring her anything, I should bring bread and pea-nut butter so she can make a new sandwich," I said.

"Groceries? No, that won't do at all!" Mémère said. "It might look like we think the child's poor, and that'd be insulting."

"But she *is* poor. Isn't she?" I thought that's why migrant workers kept moving, because they didn't have enough money and needed to find work—even if it was far away.

"Tigerlily Marie!" Mémère said.

I cringed. When Mémère uses my whole, real name like that, the conversation is over. Because Mémère is the only person who hates my name as much as I do.

The story is that when Mama looked out the hospital window right after I was born, she saw orange tiger lilies blooming. It was such a pretty sight; she picked my name right then and there.

I wish Mama had seen roses or violets or daisies out the window that day. But as Pépère always says, there's sunshine on the other side of every rain cloud. So it could've been worse. Mama could've named me Ragweed.

Lucky jumped up when he heard us walking toward the door. "Go lie down!" Mémère said. "You've caused enough trouble today."

Lucky flopped on his dog bed under the window. If Pépère or I had scolded him, Lucky would've whimpered and wrinkled his brow into the saddest dog face ever, trying to change our minds. But those tricks didn't work with Mémère.

A long time ago, he was Mama's dog. Pépère says Maine was never enough for her, and after high school, Mama went off to Boston and then Florida and then New York. But I guess those places weren't enough, either, because she came back, bringing Lucky and me with her.

I wish I knew what Mémère said when Mama came home with a puppy and a two-year-old. Even though I was there, I don't remember that day or anything about being two. I don't even remember Mama—except for photos I've seen or stories people have told me. To me, Mémère and Pépère's apartment above the store has always been home, Mama has always been gone, and Lucky has always been grown-up—and now, old.

I didn't even know he was losing his sight. Dr. Katz said it had come on slowly and there was nothing I could've done to stop it. Still, when something bad is happening to your best friend, it seems like you should know.

"I'll be back," I promised Lucky. Then I followed Mémère downstairs from our home above the store.

I shifted my feet, waiting while she put a frozen pork pie in a paper bag.

"It's a nice night," Pépère said. "So we'll walk."

I sighed. If we took the truck, the whole embarrassing trip would be over quicker, but he only used the truck when he had to. Gas is expensive and the truck is old.

"Be safe," Mémère said, as usual.

It's a long walk to the barrens, especially if it's the *second* time you've had to take that trip in one day. On the way, I took extra steps to keep up with Pépère. We walked quietly out of town and down the road that cuts the barrens in half, past all the NO TRESPASSING signs and toward the line of little blue cabins for the workers at Winthrop Blueberry.

Coming along, the migrant camp just seems to pop up suddenly in the middle of the wide, flat barrens. It always reminds me of *The Wizard of Oz* when the Emerald City appears in the distance over the poppy fields. Except the camp buildings are blue, not emerald green, and there's a big group of orange Porta Potties in the center.

As we left the road, there was another sign, ALL VISITORS MUST REGISTER AT THE SECURITY BUILDING. I'd never actually gone into the camp before. I swallowed hard as we passed men smoking cigarettes around a picnic table. A few of them turned to look at us, like Pépère and I didn't belong there. I wished I could just stash the bag with the pork pie behind one of the towers of empty blueberry bins so I wouldn't have to give the girl this ridiculous thank-you present.

"The girl who helped you was Hispanic?" Pépère asked me quietly.

I nodded.

"Miguel might know her, and he speaks English," Pépère said.

The migrant workers mostly keep to themselves, but they all get to know Mémère and Pépère eventually. Our store is the closest one to the camp, and we can wire money to faraway places. So they come in to send some of their paychecks home to Mexico or Honduras or Quebec or wherever the rest of their family lives. Helping out at the store, I know some of the workers who come each year to live in those tiny blue houses. There's Charles Wabisi, a Micmac from Nova Scotia, and the Perez family, who stays through December to work at the Christmas wreath–making factory. Diego Perez is in my class at school until holiday break every year. We have a going-away party for him before he leaves each winter.

And there's Miguel, who brings the blueberry rakes to Pépère any time they need fixing.

Only some of the workers speak English. If they're from Canada, sometimes they speak French, but Pépère has no trouble with that. He can switch between French and English in the middle of a sentence—sometimes without even meaning to. Both of us know only a handful of words in Spanish, though. And *gracias* was the only word I thought would be helpful right now.

"Miguel?" Pépère asked the men at the picnic table. A man in a black T-shirt pointed to the office, a bigger building than the cabins, but painted the same blue with white trim.

Sure enough, we saw Miguel as soon as we stepped inside. He was standing beside a desk, helping another man fill out some paperwork.

"Excuse me, Miguel?" Pépère said.

Miguel and the man looked up. "Armand!" he said, smiling. "What can I do for you?"

I hoped Pépère would explain, but he pushed the back of my arm. "Lily needs a little help."

I took a deep breath. "My dog got loose today and ran all the way here. A girl who was raking helped me catch him, and my dog ate her peanut-butter sandwich. Mémère thought Mrs. Lamont's pork pie would be a better thank-you present than another sandwich, though. So I brought one."

I knew I was babbling because the man with Miguel was looking back at his paperwork. He'd already given up trying to understand me.

"I don't know how to find the girl because I don't know her name," I continued.

"Where was she raking?" Miguel asked.

"Near the road," I said.

"Yes, but where?" he asked. "The fields were lined with string for raking. If you could tell me where, I might know which family had that section."

"I could show you," I said.

Miguel and Pépère and the man with the paperwork trailed behind me, until I was pretty sure I had the right area.

"I'd guess it was the Santiagos. Cottage number fifty-seven." Miguel pointed down the row of little blue cabins. "Their daughter's name is Salma."

I hesitated. It was one thing to tell Mémère I'd do this and another thing to walk up to the Santiagos' cabin and hand over a pork pie.

"Come on," Miguel said. "I'll introduce you."

That made me feel a little better. Pépère and I followed Miguel past campers and trucks and lots of little blue houses, some with picnic tables and others with boxes and coolers beside the door. In the dirt driveway between #57 and #58 was an older green pickup truck with Florida license plates and some trash cans with the lids tied down to keep the raccoons and bears and seagulls from helping themselves.

My heart beat hard as Miguel knocked on the door. A man with a dark mustache answered, squinting a little, looking worried when he saw us. Miguel spoke to the man in Spanish, and the man said, "Salma?"

Miguel nodded. "Eduardo, this is Armand Dumont who runs the general store in town with his wife, Marie," he said in English, "and here is their granddaughter, Lily."

"Hello," said Pépère. "Nice to meet you."

"Come in," the man said.

Whew. He speaks some English. But as I followed him inside, I couldn't help staring. On the outside, the cabin was painted light blue with white trim, as cute as a dollhouse. But inside there were only four bare wood walls, the beams all showing. Hats and shirts hung on nails, and bunk beds lined two of the walls. A table and chairs took up the opposite corner. A woman sat in one of the chairs. She had long brown hair and she stood up as we entered, smoothing the sides of her jeans. A radio played quietly on the table next to a roll of paper towels, a gallon jug of water, and a little pile of upside-down playing cards, like we'd interrupted a game.

"This is Rosa Santiago," Miguel said, motioning to the woman. "And their daughter, Salma."

Salma was sitting on one of the bottom bunk beds, her feet up on the bed, her arms hugging her knees.

My hands twisted the edge of the bag. *Smile*, I told myself.

"Hi." Salma stood up and crossed her arms over her stomach. "How's your dog?"

"He's fine." I pulled in a deep breath. "I wanted to say thank you—gracias—for giving my dog your lunch today. I don't know how I would've caught him if you hadn't. And he's blind, so he would've been in trouble if he'd reached the woods. He doesn't bump into stuff at home, because he's memorized everything—well, unless we forget and move something—but he definitely would've hurt himself here if he'd run into a tree. But anyway, I felt bad that, um, maybe you didn't get to eat any lunch, because Lucky ate yours. So I wanted to bring you something to make up for that, and my grandmother thought you might like this pie. It's called tourtière—that's French.

But it's not dessert pie. It's dinner pie, with pork. So I hope you aren't vegetarian."

Mrs. Santiago asked something in Spanish and Salma answered her.

I wish I knew enough to translate what they'd said to each other, because I worried it was something like this:

Who is this crazy girl and what does she want?

I have no idea. Something about pie.

"Mrs. Lamont makes them," I continued. "And they're kind of famous—well, in the pork pie world."

The pork pie world? I should just stop talking.

"Bake it for forty-five minutes at 350 degrees," Pépère added. "The instructions are on the bottom."

As he spoke, I suddenly realized the cabin didn't have a whole kitchen. Just some boxes and cans of food stacked up in plastic crates near the table. I'd brought something for her family to cook and they had no stove. They didn't even have a refrigerator to store it in. I didn't dare look at anyone as I set the pork pie on the table beside the playing cards. "Anyway, gracias," I said, but I was so nervous it came out sounding more like "gracious."

Salma said something to her parents in Spanish, but

as I walked away, she spoke in English. "Thank you for the famous pork pie."

Was she making fun of me? But when I turned to look, she wasn't smirking. Arms down by her sides, she was smiling.

I didn't even have to tell my face to smile back—it did it all by itself.

"I'm really glad your dog is okay," she said.

I nodded. "Me too. But you're the reason he's okay—well, you and your *sandwich.*"

"And don't forget the chips!" she said.

None of the adults seemed to think that was funny. But Salma and I laughed like it was the funniest joke ever.

As I walked out of the camp with Pépère, I turned around every few feet to wave to Salma standing in the doorway of #57.

She waved back, until the road took us out of sight.

Chapter 3

Early the next morning, I helped Mémère bake blueberry pies upstairs while Pépère went down to open the store, make the coffee, and take care of the first customers.

In the summer, our store gets lots of business. But after the blueberry barrens turn from summer blue and green to fiery autumn red, things slow down. By the time the snow comes and winter settles in to stay, we get only a trickle of locals and snowmobilers.

So Mémère and Pépère have to make most of their money from June to early October when the bell above the door is constantly ringing with all kinds of people coming in: workers from the blueberry fields, Canadian tourists driving south, American tourists driving north, summer people, lost people needing directions, and locals.

As Pépère says, "It takes all kinds of people to make a world," and our store is the only one in town, so everyone comes here. Blueberry pies and muffins are big sellers, so Mémère and I bake lots of them.

Lucky lay in his hopeful spot under the kitchen table where he always likes to be when we're eating or baking— just in case something drops. While Mémère had her back to me, I pinged a blueberry off the side of the table on purpose, so he wouldn't be disappointed.

Even though he couldn't see it, Lucky was on that blueberry like a seagull on a French fry. His eyes used to be black with a twinkle in them, but now they're blue-ish gray. They don't even look like they belong to him. It's like someone just traded out his sparkling black eyes and left blue marbles instead.

"I haven't seen much of Hannah this summer." Mémère pushed a strand of graying hair away from her face. "What's she been up to?"

I shrugged. "Probably helping her dad."

"Have you called her?" Mémère asked. "Because—"

"I will," I said quickly. I didn't want to explain that it isn't as fun with Hannah anymore. Or how it makes me sad because I miss the way it used to be.

Hannah and I had become friends on the first day of kindergarten when she shared her chocolate cookies with me at snack time. From then on, Pépère said we were like two peas in a pod.

But last year toward the end of fifth grade, something shifted, and I don't know how to fix it. I'm not sure how it happened, but it was like a crack that started small and kept getting bigger and bigger.

Before I knew it, there was only one pea left in the pod. I still love to do the things Hannah and I always did together: riding bikes, hiking, swimming, and playing with Lucky. Hannah still likes those things sometimes, but they aren't her favorites anymore. Now she mostly wants to talk about the boy from church that she secretly likes—though it's only a secret to *him*. We don't go to the same church, so I've never met the Amazing Brandon. But if she talked *to* him half as much as she talks *about* him, she'd have talked his ear off by now.

By the time Mémère and I finished baking, our whole kitchen smelled sweet and blue. Mémère loaded up pie baskets so we could each carry four pies downstairs to the store.

"Come on, Lucky!" I said. "Let's go to work!"

"Lucky should stay—" Mémère started, but he was already beside the door, waiting for me. His wagging tail whipped the hem of Mémère's skirt as she stepped past him. Lucky didn't see her frown.

Pépère says Mémère is "practical to a fault." That means she likes everything to make sense and to do its job. And Lucky doesn't really fit that. He doesn't earn his keep, the way a farm animal might. She doesn't see the point of him.

But I think the real reason Mémère doesn't like Lucky is because she blames him for Mama being gone. They had a fight about Lucky one night and Mama left, slamming the door, leaving a hole behind her as wide as the whole world.

If Pépère and I didn't love Lucky so much, I think Mémère would've given him away a long time ago. But as Pépère says to me, "We outnumber her." So Lucky stays.

I counted to twenty-five in my head to give Mémère a big head start down the stairs before saying again, "Come on, Lucky. Let's go to work!"

I always go ahead of him on the stairs, because it's easier for him to follow the sound of my footsteps than to step off into empty space.

Downstairs, Mémère was already talking to Charles Wabisi, who was buying cans of beans and tomato sauce. I left my baskets behind the counter so Mémère could decide which pies went in the display case and which ones went in the freezer. Then I led Lucky right to my table by the coffee station.

Our store is a true general store: a little of this and a little of that, adding up to a whole lot of everything. You can buy candy, souvenirs, local foods and artwork, garden supplies, car stuff, and more. The sign above the cash register says, IF WE DON'T HAVE IT, YOU DON'T NEED IT.

But mostly, we *do* have it.

The store's a mishmash of smells, too: soaps and balsam and a big pot of coffee brewing in the corner. When I'm in the store, it also smells like lumber and paint, because Pépère builds houses for mason bees and I paint them. I work at a little table near the coffee station, because that's where you hear all the news in town.

When most people think of bees, they think of honeybees that live in hives, but mason bees don't live that way. Mason bees are little, native bees. They don't mind living near one another, but—unlike honeybees that share the work—mason bees are solitary. They aren't yellow and black, either—they're blue! Tiny blue bees that just fly about, minding their own business, pollinating the blueberry barrens and people's gardens. They live in holes, not hives, so Pépère takes a fat block of wood, about the size of a hardcover book, and drills lots of little holes in the skinny side. I stencil the front with paint to make it pretty. Pépère calls my painting "bee-dazzling."

Every time we sell a bee house, Pépère takes out enough money to buy the materials, and the rest goes to me. I'm saving up to pay for an operation on Lucky's eyes so maybe he'll be able to see again. It'll take me a long time to earn enough, but as Pépère says, "Every little bit helps, and even the ocean is made up of drops."

I have three different patterns: blueberries and blue bees, green grass with pink flowers, or a circle of maple leaves that I usually paint autumn red, orange, yellow, and brown because those colors sell better than green.

Which one should I choose today? Looking through my stencils, I wondered if Mémère was right and maybe I should call Hannah. Part of me wanted to.

"She's over by the coffee," I heard Mémère say. "Lily!"

I looked up from my stencil to see Salma Santiago standing by the register.

I jumped to my feet so fast that I woke Lucky under the table. He barked.

"Shh," I said, grabbing his collar. "It's okay. I was just surprised."

"Hey," Salma said, coming over. "The pork pie was good. We all tried it." She laid something wrapped in waxed paper on my painting table. "My mama sent you a blueberry enchilada."

My first thought popped right out of my mouth. "How'd she cook it without a stove?" I blushed, hoping I hadn't offended her.

"There's a camp kitchen," Salma said matter-of-factly. "Everyone can use it, and Mama sometimes bakes things to sell."

Salma seemed to be waiting for me to try the enchilada, so I unwrapped the waxed paper. Folded up tight, the enchilada was like a little package and still warm. I didn't know if I'd like it, so I took just a small bite from the corner. It was as gooey and sweet as blueberry pie, but just a little spicy, too.

"It's really good!" It felt wrong to eat in front of her. So I grabbed a couple of napkins and a stirrer from the coffee station. "We'll split it."

As I sawed through the enchilada with the coffee stirrer, Salma touched Lucky's head.

His whole body startled, bumping the table leg.

"Just say his name first," I told her. "He likes being patted, but it surprises him if he doesn't know it's coming."

"Hey, Lucky," she said softly, reaching out her hand.

As soon as Lucky sniffed her fingers, his tail thumped happily on the floor.

"He remembers you." I handed Salma her half of the enchilada.

She broke off a piece and held it in front of Lucky's nose. He only took one sniff before gulping it down so fast I don't think he even chewed it, more like he breathed it down.

"I used to have a dog," Salma said. "Her name was Luna because she was bright white. Even outside in the dark you could see her, just like the moon."

"Lucky is the exact opposite," I said. "He blends in with the dark. A few times, I've tripped over him when I had to get up in the night."

"Maybe Luna and Lucky would've been friends," Salma said, smiling.

I shook my head. "I can't let Lucky play with other dogs. He can't see if they're happy or angry. So he might do the wrong thing and get hurt."

"Wouldn't he know from listening to the other dog?" Salma asked.

"Maybe," I said. "But what if he couldn't tell?"

As Salma rubbed his ears, Lucky's tongue moved all around, trying to lick her fingers. "I wish we could get another dog," Salma said. "But Papa thinks it's too hard when we're away from home so much."

I didn't want to hurt her by asking about something sad, but I *was* wondering. "What happened to Luna?"

Salma didn't look at me, just kept rubbing Lucky's ears. "We left her with my grandma while we were away last summer. Luna dug under her fence and escaped. I think maybe she went back to our house looking for us. But no one was home. Whenever I see a white dog, I check to see if it's her."

Lucky rested his chin on Salma's knee to make it easier for her to pat him.

My stomach hurt thinking about never seeing my dog again. "If you hadn't stopped Lucky with your lunch, I might've lost him, too."

Salma nodded. "That's why I ran so fast."

I don't know many kids who've lost somebody really important to them. Usually I'm the only one. It felt good to meet someone who knew that "missing" feeling, too.

"Lucky's from Florida," I told her. "My mama lived there before I was born."

"Lucky, you're from Florida, too? Just like me?" Then Salma spoke to him in Spanish, soft and pretty.

He did a little half jump to put his front paws in her lap. Maybe he knew what she said. Or maybe he just heard the friendship in her voice. Or maybe there are some things a dog just understands.

As Salma scratched Lucky's chest, she looked over at my paints and half-finished bee house. "What are you doing?"

"I'm painting houses for mason bees," I explained. "Mason bees are tiny blue bees that live in holes. So my pépère—that's my grandfather—he makes these houses and I bee-dazzle them. That's what Pépère calls it when I decorate them. We sell them here in the store. I'm saving up money for an operation to help Lucky's eyes."

"What's wrong with his eyes?" Salma held another bite of enchilada close to Lucky's nose, and he gobbled it up.

"He has something called cataracts. It's why his eyes look cloudy. Our vet said Lucky might still be able to see shadows, but we don't know for sure. My mémère says the operation is too expensive and maybe it won't even work and blind dogs adjust fine. But I figure if I pay for it myself, she can't say no."

Salma picked up one of my paintbrushes. "I'm good at painting. I'll help you."

"Really? Okay." It would be nice to have help. "Lucky, get down now," I said, pulling him off Salma's lap so she could choose a stencil. "Do you want to paint blueberries, flowers, or leaves?"

"Flowers, but I don't need the stencil." Salma reached

into my paint case. My eyebrows shot up as she took my fall maple leaf orange and grass green and flower pink.

"Are you going to use those *together*?" I asked.

"It'll be beautiful." She took a pencil and divided the square front of the bee house into six equal-size boxes. Then she started painting the boxes different colors: green, pink, and orange along the top; blue, red, and yellow on the bottom.

Molly Peasley came to the coffee station. She glanced over at us and then took a step backward. I don't know if it was the bright colors of Salma's bee house or Salma herself sitting at my little table that seemed so surprising.

By then Salma's first square was dry. On the green background, she painted an orange circle with red petals and dots of yellow in the middle. A flower so vibrant and bold and big that it nearly filled the square. On the pink square, she painted a green circle with yellow petals and dots of blueberry blue.

Her bee house wouldn't fit in with mine. But what was I supposed to say?

"I wish I'd brought my paints with me from home, but I didn't think we'd be gone this long," Salma said. "A family that usually comes to Maine couldn't come this year, and they offered us their spot. So we went right from Pennsylvania to here. Maine isn't as cold as I expected it to be. And I haven't seen one lighthouse yet!" Salma sighed. "They're on all the postcards, but where are they?"

"It's only cold in Maine in the winter," I explained. "And we have a few lighthouses near us, but they're on islands. You can only see them down at the point. Or if you're in a boat."

"Oh." Salma painted a blue flower with pink petals in the orange square.

Funny to think she expected to see lighthouses around every bend in the road. But I guess if you've never been here, you might think that. I went back to my stencil, and Molly Peasley went back to her coffee. Lucky slept on the floor next to Salma, his head on her foot.

When Salma and I were done painting, I placed the bee houses on the shelf above my table, facing out, so they could finish drying. Anyone who walked by that shelf would see four bee houses: three of my stenciled blueberries and bees, and Salma's flower-power color explosion.

"You should sign yours," Salma said. "Artists sign their work."

I'd been so distracted by the flowers that I hadn't noticed the tiny word SALMA painted down in the bottom corner.

"It's just stenciling," I said as I put up the little sign that I always used when the bee houses weren't ready for sale. THESE MASON BEE HOUSES ARE DRYING, BUT THERE ARE MORE IN THE GARDENING SECTION!

Salma stood back to admire them. "After I'm done raking tomorrow, I could come and help you paint again. The more bee houses you have for sale, the more money you'll make for Lucky's eyes."

I opened my mouth, but I couldn't tell her the truth. I couldn't afford to waste bee houses, and I didn't think anyone would buy Salma's bee-double-dazzled one. It was just too colorful and loud. Who would want that in their garden? The bees might even be scared of it.

I liked Salma, though, and I really did want her to come back. So I said, "Gracias," and didn't mention that I planned to paint over her bee house after it dried.

Chapter 4

The next morning, when I came downstairs to the store, Salma's bee house wasn't on the drying shelf.

The sign was still there. All my bee houses were lined up on the shelf—just as I'd left them. But Salma's was gone.

Beside me, Caleb Dow and Jacob Dunlap were fixing their coffee at the coffee station. "I know!" Caleb said to Jacob as he poured sugar into his cup. "If the town had fixed it right the first time—Good morning, Lily—we wouldn't *be* in this mess."

"Hey, Lucky!" Jacob ran his hand over Lucky's head before picking up a little wooden coffee stirrer. "Didn't I tell you that? It's gonna cost *twice* as much because they tried to cut corners."

As soon as I had Lucky settled under my table, I turned and headed for the front of the store, bumping Caleb on my way.

"Careful, Lily! This is hot."

Pépère was ringing up Mrs. Putney buying some milk. Usually I wouldn't interrupt, but—"Pépère, one of the bee houses that was drying is missing! Do you have it?"

He grinned. "Do you mean that razzle-bee-dazzled one? I sold it!"

My mouth dropped open. "You *sold* it? To who?"

"Have a nice day now!" Pépère said to Mrs. Putney. "I hope your company enjoys their trip to Bar Harbor. You tell them to get there early. It can be hard to find parking downtown in the afternoon."

I squeezed my lips shut, waiting for her to leave. But as soon as I heard the bell ring over the door, the words rushed out, "Who bought the bee house?"

"I don't know the lady's name," Pépère said. "Just a tourist passing through. She came in to pay for her gasoline and she saw that fancy bee house. She wanted it bad. So I checked to see if the paint was dry, and it was."

"Didn't you show her the others?" I asked. "The ones for sale up by the gardening supplies?"

"I did, but she had her heart set on that flashy one. She called it art."

I felt a little sour that the lady didn't think *mine* were art. Still, a sale was a sale. Every bit of money was a help.

When three o'clock came, Lucky knew Salma was there before I did. Maybe he could smell her or maybe he already knew her footsteps. But I heard his tail thump on the floor under my table.

"Hi, Lucky!" As Salma patted his head, he wagged all over. Even his tongue swung back and forth with happiness.

"We sold the bee house you painted yesterday," I said. "In fact, Pépère sold it before it was even for sale. The lady who bought it really liked it."

"That's great!" Salma said. "This morning while I was raking, I saw some of those little blue mason bees. They put me in the mood to paint bees today."

I handed her the blue paint, but Salma said, "No, thanks. My bees are gonna be pink."

Pink? I opened my mouth, but she was already opening the pink paint. Just because one lady had liked Salma's crazy-colored bee house didn't mean I could sell more of them. Flowers came in lots of colors, but bees—"Have you ever seen a pink bee?" I asked.

Salma nodded. "Sure. In my imagination. Don't you like to imagine?"

"Sometimes," I said slowly. My favorite thing to pretend was that Mama was behind me, invisible to everyone else. Every now and then she'd whisper things in my ear, things like "I'm proud of you" when I did good in school. Or "You look as pretty as the tiger lilies I saw on that first day," when I'm dressing up for church. Things Mémère didn't ever say even if maybe she thought so.

I picked up my paintbrush. "I've never imagined pink bees." Especially with orange stripes.

"I imagine all the time," Salma said. "That's how I keep work from being boring. Raking blueberries is buggy, and sometimes it's so hot that sweat is dripping all over me by the time we're done."

We both made a face.

"But when you pretend, life can be any way you want it to be," she added. "So I imagine it better. Today I imagined I was a princess and the fields were really my lands. But an evil queen cast a spell over everyone so we all had to pick her blueberries." She smiled at me. "Tell me a chore that you hate to do, and I'll show you how to imagine it better."

"Um," I said, trying to think of something really bad. "Picking up dog poop in the yard?"

Salma giggled. "That's a hard one. Maybe you could imagine it's something wonderful that you're picking up? Seashells? Or treasure? Or Easter eggs."

"Easter eggs?" I asked. We both burst out laughing.

"Okay, maybe that's too weird," Salma admitted. "But you see what I mean."

Watching her paint blue daisies for her pink-and-orange bees, I wondered how she could just pick colors and have faith they'd look good together.

I looked down at the blueberry stencil taped to the front of my bee house. Maybe I could try stenciling

the leaves red, like they turn in the fall? Just for something different? But if the leaves were red, it would be
autumn. There wouldn't be any berries on the plants. It
wouldn't make sense.

I picked up the green paint and went to work.

Chapter 5

Dr. Katz liked to say she had no choice but to become a veterinarian. With a name like "Katz" everyone expects you to like cats, so it was good that she did. It was good for Lucky and me that she also liked dogs and kids.

She was one of the only people I ever let call me Tigerlily, because she said it like it was pretty.

Dr. Katz went to high school with Mama. When she tells me stories about Mama, somehow I never feel bad for asking her to remember something that turned out sad. And when Lucky's eyes clouded over last year, she put her arm around me and said, "It'll be okay, Tigerlily. Blind dogs learn to get along."

I didn't want Lucky to just get along—I wanted him to see. So Dr. Katz promised she'd check with a friend who operates on animals' eyes and find out how much it would cost. "Even with the operation, there are no guarantees," she told me. "And it's harder on an old dog to go through surgery. There are risks."

Those were reasons enough for Mémère to say no. She said she knew someone who had a blind dog that could hear a Cheeto hit the floor clear across the room and never bumped into anything unless they changed the furniture around. That dog still barked at squirrels because he could hear and smell them, even if he couldn't see them.

But learning not to bump into things seemed like a poor trade for seeing. And hearing squirrels but not chasing them and watching them run away just felt like losing. Only having half of something after you've had it all is a special kind of sadness.

I cried about it, until one night Pépère came in and sat on my bed with me. "You never know what you can do until you try," he said, and we came up with the idea of selling bee houses. If I earned the money myself, Mémère couldn't say it was too expensive.

Sundays and Thursdays were Dr. Katz's days off. On Sundays, I had church and then I had to help out at home. But every nice Thursday, I made sure to walk Lucky by Dr. Katz's house, just in case she was outside in her garden. I always felt a little guilty, because I was hoping she'd stop what she was doing and check Lucky's eyes for free.

Mémère would stop me if she knew. She says we don't need charity.

Dr. Katz never makes it feel like charity, though. She likes Lucky and wants him to be happy, just like I do.

On this Thursday, Dr. Katz's car was in her driveway and I could see her bent over her flowers in the backyard. I pulled on Lucky's leash so we'd be in front of her house as long as possible. "Nice day!" I called.

She stood and looked over. "It *is* a lovely day! Tigerlily, can you stop for a minute? I have something for you."

Lucky's head shot up and his tail wagged hard. He loves Dr. Katz. But on the way up her walkway, he lifted his leg on her petunias.

"No!" I said, but some things can't be stopped.

"A dog's gotta do what a dog's gotta do. Isn't that right, Lucky?" Dr. Katz smiled at me. "What I have for you is on the kitchen table. Do you want to come in?"

"How about if I just wait here?" I was afraid if I walked Lucky to her house, he'd pee on every plant on the way. Or maybe even leave an Easter egg or two.

When Dr. Katz came back outside, she had something small and square in her hand. "My dad has been cleaning out some old boxes, and he found a few of my high school scrapbooks. Your mom was in these two photos. I thought you might like to have them."

My heart jumped. I've seen all the photos that Mémère and Pépère have of Mama. Christmas photos. School photos. Graduation photos. Mama with me and Lucky.

But here were two photos that I'd never seen.

Dr. Katz handed me the first one. "This was taken on a school field trip that our high school class took to Boston. We were in the Public Garden. Your mom is wearing the red shirt."

I saw her even before Dr. Katz pointed her out. I would've known Mama anywhere. But this photo wasn't posed like some of the other photos I'd seen. Here she just looked relaxed and happy, standing in front of a big tree with some friends.

Dr. Katz passed me the second photo. "And this was one of the years she won Downeast Blueberry Queen. I'm sorry I don't remember which year."

There was Mama with her blonde hair done up fancy, wearing her dark blue sparkly dress and big silver and blue crown. Mama won the Downeast Blueberry Queen Pageant three years running, and no one has done that since. She holds the record.

I like that Mama has something special that people still talk about. The blueberry festival happens every year in late August, and it's a big deal around here. Our corner of Maine doesn't have as many tourists and events and stores full of expensive things, like you might find elsewhere along the coast. But we produce the most wild blueberries, and that's Maine's state fruit. So the festival is our chance to celebrate that. The pageant starts the festival and the queen represents our area at events all over Maine. So it's a big honor to win.

"This photo was taken the second time Mama won," I said. "I can tell from the dress she's wearing. Mémère and Pépère have photos from each year."

But they didn't have this one. Here she was standing with another girl, and Mama had an expression on her face that I'd never seen before. Mama had a glint in her eyes and one side of her smile was higher than the other—like maybe she was thinking about some mischief. It tore at me inside. "Who's she with?" I asked.

Dr. Katz grinned. "Can you guess?"

I looked closer. The girl's hair was really long in the photo, but there was something familiar about her face. "Wait. Is that *you*? You were pretty." I blushed. "I mean, um, you *are*—"

Dr. Katz held up her hand. "Your mom was the pretty one. But that's not what I admired about her. No French Canadian girl had ever won blueberry queen, and Danielle set out to challenge that. I remember her saying that she'd show them all. And she did."

"She showed them *three* times," I said.

"Yes!" Dr. Katz said. "Your mom wasn't afraid to think big thoughts. That's what I admired most about her."

I wished I could be big-thinking, too. Things happen to people like that—good things and bad things. But even a few bad things might be better than no things happening to you.

Sometimes I wondered what Mama would have thought of me. Deep inside, I was afraid she might've been disappointed that I wasn't more like her.

I felt such a rush of feelings that my hand shook sliding the photos into my shorts' pocket. "Thank you so much" was all I could say.

"You're welcome, Tigerlily. Now, let me have a quick look at Lucky's eyes." Dr. Katz cupped her hand under his chin and lifted his head to examine him. "How's he doing?"

"I think he's getting blinder." My voice dropped to a whisper without me even telling it to.

"Really, if you think about it, it's probably kinder to him that it's coming on slowly." Dr. Katz looked carefully at each eye. "Imagine how terrible it would be to wake up blind one day and not know why. This way, he gets used to it in stages."

"He remembers where things are at home. And he goes up and down the aisles at the store pretty well, unless there are lots of people," I explained. "But on the stairs and in a new place he waits for me to go first."

"Smart dog," Dr. Katz said.

"Except once this week he didn't hold back at all!" I said. "I was taking him for a walk and he got loose on the blueberry barrens, and I couldn't get him to stop. I kept thinking he'd run smack into the trees if he made it to the woods. Then a Winthrop truck came along! I was so scared that he'd dart out in front of it."

Dr. Katz grimaced. "How'd you catch him?"

"Salma—one of the kids from the blueberry camp—stopped him. Well, actually, her *lunch* stopped him!"

Dr. Katz laughed, ruffling Lucky's ears. "Must've been a good lunch. I'm sure it was scary, but Lucky doesn't look any worse for the experience. In fact, he's quite healthy for his age, considering everything."

"Did you find out how much that eye operation costs?"

Dr. Katz sighed. "My friend said he'd give me a break on the price, but there are still follow-up exams, medications, and lab tests, on top of the surgery. All that together is over two thousand dollars, even with the discount."

I felt everything inside me crashing to the ground. That was so much. "I'm painting mason bee houses to earn the money, but it'll take me awhile," I said. "A long while."

Dr. Katz nodded. Then she smiled. "I didn't even know that mason bees lived in houses."

Funny to think I knew something about animals that she didn't. But no one brings bees into a vet. "They're great pollinators. They're good for the blueberry fields, but also good for regular gardens. And they live in holes, so Pépère makes the bee houses with lots of little, bee-size holes in the side. Then I paint the houses to make them pretty."

"I need some bee houses for my garden. Do you sell them at the store?"

"Oh, you don't have to *buy* one," I said quickly. "I could give you one."

"No, of course I want to buy one. Or maybe a few. Bees are very important to a garden."

She seemed sure. "I do have three different styles to choose from," I explained. "Blueberries and bees, flowers, and maple leaves. Oh, and then there's a fourth style that I didn't paint—Salma did. Her bee house has *pink* bees."

Dr. Katz smiled. "Pink bees?"

I nodded. "It's different."

"Different can be good," Dr. Katz said. "It makes you pay attention."

On the walk back to the store, I kept reaching into my pocket to touch the hard edges of the photos. I couldn't wait to show them to Mémère and Pépère. But when I got back to the store, Pépère was busy with a customer, and Mémère told me that a family from Connecticut had bought Salma's bee house, along with a bundle of firewood for their camp and one of our blueberry pies. "The woman gave me her phone number," Mémère said. "She'd like a few more bee houses to give as presents."

"Did you show her the ones in the gardening section?" I asked.

"I did, but she liked the style of the one she bought," Mémère said. "So when we have some more of those to sell, we should give her a call."

I didn't feel like sharing the photos anymore. Every bee house we sold meant more money for Lucky, but I couldn't help wondering if the lady would've bought some of my bee houses if Salma's hadn't been there, outshining mine.

Making mine too ordinary to be noticed.

Chapter 6

Early the next afternoon, I looked up from painting to see my friend Hannah coming up the store aisle, carrying a bunch of empty grocery bags. "Hi, Lily!" she said.

I smiled, but my mouth stayed closed. I used to feel a hundred percent happy when I saw her, but now there's always a little bit of doubt mixed in.

Lucky only felt happy, though. His tail wagged so hard it's a wonder his whole back end didn't lift off in the air like a helicopter. He has always loved Hannah.

I'd hardly seen her since school let out in June. Her dad's a lobsterman and she helps out on his boat in the summertime. But she doesn't have to work on Sundays and stormy days, and I hadn't even seen her on *those* days.

As Hannah patted Lucky, I glanced out the store window to see if a lightning storm had rolled in while I was busy painting. Nope, just blue sky and sunshine. "How come you're off today?"

"My grandpa had a doctor's appointment, and he needed my dad to drive him," she said. "They invited me to go, but that didn't sound like much fun. So Mom asked me to pick some bags of sea lavender. She wants to make some wreaths to sell at the blueberry festival. Want to ride your bike down the boat landing with me and help? Mom said there are some patches of sea lavender growing right there."

I looked at the clock over the door. It was already one o'clock. Would Salma come today? I didn't want to miss her.

But if I said no, Hannah might not try again. Maybe I could go with Hannah and be back before Salma got here.

"Okay," I said. "Let me put Lucky upstairs."

In the past, he could've run alongside my bike, but now I couldn't risk him running into my wheels. It's one of the things I can't wait to do again after his operation— Lucky running beside my bike, both of us speeding along the back roads.

"Oh, Lucky," Hannah said as he pushed his nose into her hand. "Lily, if we walked, could he come?"

I sucked my bottom lip. Walking would take longer. But Lucky was so happy to see Hannah . . . I could write Salma a note, just in case I was late.

"That'll work," I said. "Would you run upstairs and get Lucky's l-e-a-s-h for me? It's where we usually keep it. I just need to leave a note."

I had to hold Lucky's collar to keep him from following Hannah. He whimpered. "She'll be right back," I said to comfort him, but when someone leaves, Lucky doesn't know if they're going for one minute or forever.

With my free hand, I reached over to the coffee station for a napkin to write on.

I went for a walk with Lucky to help a friend, but a lady bought your pink bees house! She said she wanted a few more. So if you want to paint today,

I've left everything here for you. I'll be back as soon as I can!

I set up the paints and brushes and stacked two blank bee houses on my table.

On our way out, I told Mémère, "I'm going for a walk with Hannah and Lucky to the boat landing."

"Be safe," Mémère said.

I rolled my eyes. She doesn't need to always say that. Really, how much trouble could I get into? Everyone who lives here knows Mémère and Pépère and me. If anything happened, word would travel so fast it'd beat me home.

Occasionally, I feel like being a smart aleck and say, "Nope, today I plan to be reckless and crazy!" Mémère doesn't think it's funny, though. It usually ends in me staying home, going nowhere.

"I will," I said.

Lucky pulled me down the road.

"So what've you been doing this summer?" I asked Hannah.

"Working a lot," she said. "But remember my friend from church, Brandon?"

Never heard of him, I wanted to say, but then she'd just start the whole story from when she met him. And I'd already heard that part a million times. "Yup."

"He and I lit the candles together at church last Sunday. I was so nervous that my hands were shaking. I was afraid I'd set the whole place on fire! Afterward, he said I'd done a great job!" She smiled.

"Wow," I said, waiting for the rest of the story. Until I realized that *was* the story.

"And next week, Mom and I are going to Boston to see my aunt Carol and get me a new dress for the blueberry festival," Hannah said.

Hannah is the reigning Downeast Blueberry Queen, but she's only won once (so far). I can cheer for Hannah to win twice, but I secretly hope she never wins a third time. Other Maine fairs and festivals have pageants: Strawberry Queen at the Hillsborough Fair, Sea Goddess at the Maine Lobster Festival. But the biggest prize and the sparkliest crown goes to the Downeast Blueberry Queen. For the past year, Hannah has worn her big silver-and-blue jeweled crown at nursing homes, at schools, in parades, and at fairs all over the state.

Ahead, a deer was crossing the road. He froze when he saw us. If he were close enough for Lucky to smell, I'd have to hold the leash tight. But the deer leaped away into the trees, his tail high.

Lucky just kept walking along.

I waited for Hannah to ask me what I'd been doing this summer so I could tell her how Lucky had run away and Salma helped me catch him and Mémère made me bring her a pork pie.

But Hannah was only thinking about the pageant. "It will be hard if I don't win Queen again. Everyone expects me to. That's the problem with winning. People expect more from you the next time. So anything less than first is failing."

"At least you get to keep the crown you already have, right?" I said, surprised that she looked so sad.

"Yeah. But it's hard just to be a regular kid after you've been someone special."

"I've always been a regular kid." I glanced at Hannah, hoping she'd say that wasn't true. Instead she told me, "You could be in the pageant, too, Lily."

I snorted. "Ha! No way. I'd probably trip and fall

across the stage, taking all the other girls down with me. We'd have a blueberry smoosh!"

We both laughed. For that moment it felt fun and easy, two peas in a pod.

"I hope Brandon comes to the pageant," Hannah said. "I want to invite him, but I'm not sure if I dare."

I think NASA should name the next black hole after Brandon. Because every conversation gets sucked down into him before long. I don't even see it coming when— *slurp!* We're gone.

"He came to the festival last year, so I was thinking I might ask him—"

I wondered what Salma would paint today. Even though her bee houses showed bees and flowers, just like mine, hers surprised you. Was that why people liked them so much? Was that why that lady called it "art"?

I sighed. I only knew how to paint things in a regular way. But we needed to sell lots of bee houses, so I hoped some people liked ordinary, too.

By the time we got to the boat landing, Lucky was letting me lead. At the boat landing, sea lavender grows wild just below the high-tide mark. It smells both sweet and salty because the tide washes in and out of it every day. It's pretty, with delicate, teeny-tiny, pale purple flowers. It dries well, so most people have a vase or a wreath of sea lavender in their homes to keep a bit of color through the winter.

Maybe I'll bring a sprig of it home with me to show Salma, I thought. She might want to paint it. I coaxed Lucky over all the rocks at the shore. "Come," I told him. "It's okay. I won't let you get hurt."

Being at the ocean feels like you're at the edge of the world with nothing but water straight ahead. It was so quiet I could hear an engine rumble, even though the boat hadn't come into view around the point yet. A cormorant was perched on a ledge marker, and little sandpipers ran along the beach, staying just out of reach of the waves.

Hannah gave me a pair of scissors and an empty bag. "Cut as low to the ground as you can so Mom'll have good stems to attach to the wreath frames, okay?"

"Okay." I looped Lucky's leash around my arm so my hands would be free.

"Thanks for helping me," Hannah said. "Last year, Mom sold wreaths at our church's booth, but this year she's renting one by herself. She has to pay a hundred dollars to rent a spot, but the wreaths don't cost much to make. And she's going to bake a bunch of blueberry pies to sell, too. She figures she'll make back her hundred dollars pretty quickly."

Was Salma still raking or was she finished by now? Was she pretending the blueberry fields belonged to a queen today? A giggle bubbled out of me, because I realized Hannah was a blueberry queen and I was cutting sea lavender for her!

"What's so funny?" Hannah asked.

"Um, I was just thinking of something."

Hannah nodded. "Brandon does this funny thing where he starts singing for no reason. It's weird, but it's also cute. One time—"

Sometimes being with someone can make you feel lonelier than if you were by yourself. I wished I could close my eyes and when I opened them, I'd be back at the store painting with Salma.

"—and he gave it to me." Hannah looked at me expectantly.

"Oh. Cool!" I said, hoping whatever he'd given her was a good thing—not the flu.

I'd had enough. "Oh, wow. I think it's getting late. I just remembered something I have to do!" I handed Hannah my full bag of sea lavender. "I hope this is enough for your mom. Wish her good luck at the festival for me, okay? Come on, Lucky. We've gotta go."

I snapped one little sprig of sea lavender to show Salma and led Lucky over all the rocks to the road. I didn't look back, afraid that Hannah might be watching us go. Was she disappointed? Or was she just thinking of Brandon?

As soon as Lucky and I were out of sight of the boat landing, we ran.

Chapter 7

When I got back to the store, Salma was already painting big and little purple circles on a bee house. She stopped to scratch Lucky behind his ears.

"Lucky, lie down." I stuck the sea lavender into a cup at the coffee station. "Sorry I wasn't here when you got here," I said. "What are you painting?"

"Blueberries. You didn't have purple paint, so I mixed red and blue." Salma dipped her paintbrush into a puddle of purple paint. "And there really *are* purple blueberries. I've seen them. So why aren't they called purpleberries?"

I shrugged. "I don't know, but wild blueberries come in lots of colors. Red, purple, pink, black, even striped sometimes. But most growers pick out any berries that aren't blue."

"Why?" Salma asked. "Do the other colors taste different?"

"No, but people think they aren't ripe unless they're blue. The different colors go into juice and wine, because then they get mashed up and strained and no one ever knows what color those berries were to start with."

"Then I'm not painting *any* blue ones," she said. "That's not fair!"

I watched her painting purple circles. They needed something to look more like real blueberries. "You should put a star on top of each one," I said.

"A star?"

"Wait here. I'll show you."

I went up to the display of blueberries for sale and picked up one box. "I'm just borrowing this for a minute," I told Mémère. "For art's sake!"

Through the plastic wrap on top of the box, I showed Salma all the little five-pointed stars, one on top of each berry. A whole box full of little blue-black stars. "Pépère said that the early Wabanakis called blueberries 'star berries.' They believed the Great Spirit sent them down from the sky once when there was no other food to eat."

"I'm going to paint yellow stars on my purpleberries so they look like stars in the sky," Salma said. "Stars are one of my favorite things. I love how when you look up at night, it doesn't matter if you're in Florida or Maine or Michigan or anywhere, it's the same stars. So when I miss someone, I look at the stars and imagine that person seeing the same ones as me. No matter where I go, I can think of them and they can think of me. They're my star friends."

Salma's head was tipped down as she painted, her long black hair shielding her face. "It must be hard to move so much," I said.

"I hate it," she said. "I don't feel like I really belong in the places we stay. And when I'm gone, my friends in Florida do things without me, and it's hard to catch up when I get back. When I come home, it's like we have to become friends all over again. Everyone changes so fast."

"I know what you mean," I said. "My friend Hannah used to be my best friend, but now all she wants to talk about is a boy she knows. She's changed so much that I don't even know how to talk to her anymore. She came to see me today and asked me to pick sea lavender with her. That's why I wasn't here when you came." I reached for the coffee cup with the sprig that I'd brought home from the boat landing. "This is what sea lavender looks like. Hannah's mom makes wreaths of it to sell at the blueberry festival."

Salma looked interested. "What's a blueberry festival?"

"Oh, it's like a fair that happens near the end of August." I put the cup back on the coffee station. "Lots of people come. There's a parade and a race and a blueberry queen pageant. And booths selling every kind of blueberry food there is: blueberry honey, blueberry tea, blueberry salad dressing, blueberry jam, blueberry pancake syrup, blueberry barbecue sauce—"

Salma made a face.

"Blueberry mustard, blueberry salsa, blueberry coffee. Not to mention all those pies and muffins. Some booths sell other things, too—like wreaths and potholders and—"

"You should sell your bee houses!" Salma said.

I shook my head. "I couldn't do that."

"Why not?" Salma asked. "I'll help you!"

"But I'd have to rent a booth," I sputtered. "And borrow a table. And probably do a bunch of other things that I don't even know about."

"The more houses you sell, the faster Lucky can have his operation," Salma said simply. "Right?"

My hands kept painting, but my mind was busy adding up the plusses and minuses.

-1. I had enough saved for the booth rent, but it didn't seem smart to give up a hundred dollars on just the hope of making more.

-2. What if no one bought anything? I would die of embarrassment.

-3. I'd never done anything like this before. I'd never even wanted to.

BUT—

+1. If I sold just four bee houses, I'd earn back enough to pay the booth rent.

+2. If I sold five, I'd be ahead. I might sell a lot more than five, too.

+3. Salma said she'd help, so I wouldn't have to do it all alone. It would be fun to run the booth together.

+4. Lucky might get his operation sooner. A lot sooner.

I looked down at him beside me, those gray-blue circles on his eyes turning the world dark. And I knew I'd try anything for Lucky—even being a big-thinker for once.

"Would you really help me?" I asked Salma quietly. "I'd need a lot of bee houses for a whole booth. And people seem to really like yours best."

"Sure." Salma held out her pinky finger. "Star friends always help each other!"

I grinned and crooked my pinkie around hers for a pinkie swear. "Yes, star friends always do."

When it was finished, Salma's bee house was covered

in different colors and sizes of blueberries, each with a yellow star on top. A bubbly, starry sky of blueberries.

The berries on my bee house were perfectly round, stenciled blue. Suddenly, they looked too plain. I picked up my littlest brush and dipped it into Salma's paint puddle. One by one, I went from blueberry to blueberry.

Adding tiny purple stars.

Chapter 8

That night at supper, I told Mémère and Pépère my plan.

"You're twelve years old!" Mémère said. "It's enough for you to sell your bee houses at the store."

I could feel myself sitting up straighter. "The more people who see them, the more chance I have to sell them," I told her.

"How are you going to get everything to the fair?" Mémère asked. "You can't take it all on your bike."

I glanced at Pépère.

"Oh no!" Mémère said, shaking her finger. "The festival is a big weekend for us at the store. I can't lose Pépère that weekend."

"We could ask someone to help out at the store," Pépère suggested.

"You think this is a good idea?" Mémère snapped at him. "That's just like you! Encouraging our kids to leap before they look. So they're never happy with what they have!"

The "our kids" hung in the air. She meant Mama and me. I looked down at Lucky on the floor beside my feet, his chest rising and falling in sleep.

"You never know what you can do until you try," Pépère said.

I lifted my eyes. He was grinning at me. I grinned back, because I knew what we were both thinking: *We outnumber her.*

Mémère must've known it, too, because she stopped arguing. "Well, it's *your* money, Lily."

And it was a lot of money. I couldn't think about it too much or I'd get scared.

The next morning, I pulled in a deep breath and took a hundred dollars out of my money jar for Lucky. I wished Salma could come with me, but she was raking and I was determined to do this. I folded the bills up to fit in my pocket, just like it was something I'd do any day.

It didn't make my pocket bulge out too far, but it felt so strange to be carrying that much money. As I walked toward town, I wondered if everyone driving by would know something about me was different.

Walking up the steps of First Parish Congregational Church, I imagined Mama behind me. She whispered in my ear, "Who cares what anyone thinks?"

Mama never did, at least that's what people say about her. Pépère said she had a laugh that carried clear across the store and everyone knew it was her. She wore long flowy skirts, even when they weren't in style.

I think beautiful people like Mama and Salma have an easier chance of getting away with being different, though. My looks must come more from my father, since no one else in my family has brown hair like me. All I know about my father is that he was a musician from New York and that's where Mama met him. Maybe if things hadn't turned out the way they did, I would be living there with Mama and him. But Mémère said he was never interested in having children.

"Good morning, Lily," said Mrs. LaRue, the church secretary. "What can I do for you, honey?"

Mrs. LaRue isn't just the church secretary; she's also one of the organizers of the blueberry festival. She's in charge of renting booths, and she's always a judge at the pageant. Some people think it's funny that we hold the pageant in a church. But it's the only building in town with enough seats.

"Um, hi, Mrs. LaRue. Is this where you can rent a booth for the blueberry festival?"

She smiled. "Yes! What are your grandparents planning to sell?"

"No." I licked my lips. "The booth is for me." I reached into my pocket and pulled out my folded money. "I have a hundred dollars. That's what it costs, right?"

Mrs. LaRue stared at the money in my hand. "Do your grandparents know you're doing this?"

I nodded firmly and passed the bills to her.

"Well, as long as you have their permission." Mrs. LaRue opened her desk drawer and took out a notebook and a receipt book. "What will you sell, dear?"

"Bee houses and maybe some food. Definitely bee houses, though. That's my main thing."

"How about if I put you down as Food and Miscellaneous?" Mrs. LaRue suggested.

I swallowed the lump in my throat. "Miscellaneous sounds good."

"You'll be booth number twenty-eight," she said. "The festival starts at nine a.m. on Saturday, but you can set up on Friday night. I recommend that you wait and bring your merchandise on Saturday, though, because no one will be there to watch over it all night. Would you like a brochure for the festival? It has the full schedule of events."

"Thank you." I took the brochure and folded it to fit in my pocket. It didn't take up as much room as all those bills.

She winked at me. "I gave you an extra good spot, but don't tell anyone, because I'm supposed to assign them in random order. See you at the festival."

Walking down the church steps, I felt like I was floating, my feet barely touching the ground. I'd really done it! Maybe Lucky could have his operation before school started!

I couldn't wait to tell Salma. I took the long road past the camp on the way home. I marched right by the NO

TRESPASSING and ALL VISITORS MUST REGISTER AT THE SECURITY BUILDING signs with my head held high to the Winthrop Blueberry office to check in.

Opening the door, I saw Mr. Winthrop himself at the coffee machine.

His eyes widened to see me.

"I'm here to see my friend Salma," I said. "She's a kid and she works here. The sign outside says I need to register."

They must not get many kids from town out visiting friends at the camp. Mr. Winthrop didn't seem to know whether he needed me to check in or not—and he's the boss! "Just go on ahead," he said.

When I knocked on the door at #57, Mrs. Santiago opened it, wearing a tank top and shorts. She put her finger to her lips. "Shh. Sleeping," she whispered.

Heat rushed to my face. Their whole cabin was only one room, so it was like I'd knocked on someone's bedroom door.

"Is Salma here?" I whispered. "It's me, Lily, the girl with the dog who brought the pork pie. Well, it wasn't the *dog* that brought the pork pie." *Why am I telling her this?*

Her dark brown eyes were kind and understanding. Maybe she wasn't following everything I said, but she was listening like it mattered.

"Lily!" Salma pushed her way past her mom. "I was just getting ready to come to the store!"

"Shh!" Mrs. Santiago said.

"My dad is taking a nap." Salma grabbed my arm. "Come on! Let's go to the playground."

I didn't even know there was a playground at the camp. I followed Salma out behind the last line of cottages to three big swing sets, the strong metal kind, like we had at our school playground. On the first set of swings, three boys were swinging standing up. Two little girls swung on the second set, so Salma and I went right for the empty third set.

"I had to come, because I couldn't wait to show you something." I pulled the brochure for the blueberry festival out of my pocket and sat down on the swing next to Salma. "I did it! I rented a booth at the festival."

Salma grinned. "That's great! Now we just have to paint as many bee houses as we can." She looked through the brochure. "Wow. I didn't know there were so many things you could do with blueberries."

In the brochure there was even a photo of Hannah wearing her sparkly blue pageant dress and her Downeast Blueberry Queen crown. She looked extra fancy with two locks of her blonde hair curled, one on each side of her face, the rest of her hair in a wispy bun. Her whole face shone with a just-won, gleaming smile.

"That's my friend Hannah," I said.

"She's pretty," Salma said, admiring.

I nodded. "The pageant is always on Friday night, and then the booths open the next day. I told Mrs. LaRue that bee houses would be our main thing, but maybe we should sell some food, too. Not everyone has a garden. But everyone likes to eat! So Mrs. LaRue wrote us down as 'Food and Miscellaneous' so we could keep our options open."

"What food would we sell?"

"Maybe blueberry pies?" I suggested. "Lots of booths sell those. And I've had plenty of practice making them with Mémère."

"But if lots of booths sell them, ours won't be special. We should make something different. Something no one else has," Salma said. "How about blueberry enchiladas? Those are good, and I bet they'd be different."

Maybe they'd be *too* different. The whole point was to make money. Salma was being really nice helping me, though, and I didn't want to hurt her feelings. "Are they hard to make?" I asked, buying myself some time to think about it.

"Easy as pie!" She laughed at her joke. "Actually they're *easier* than pie! I could show you. We can make a test batch. Can we use your kitchen?"

"Of course," I said, and immediately felt bad because she had to share a kitchen with a bunch of families. "That's no problem. Are you sure you want to help, though? You're already helping me with the bee houses."

"I'd do anything for Lucky." Salma pushed off and started swinging. "And that's what star friends do."

"Right!" I pushed off, too.

Pumping with my legs, I went higher and higher. Up, up, and *whoosh* back down. My hair rushed behind me and then in front of me.

"I'm flying!" Salma said.

"Me too!" I tried to look over at her, but my hair immediately got in the way. The ground sped past. Up I went until my toes appeared to touch the roofs of those little blue houses. Then even higher! They reached toward the far-off barrens.

Free-falling down, down. My hair streamed out in front as the ground rushed toward me, and then the swing grabbed and threw me up the other side.

I clenched my teeth. Blood rushed in my head, making my ears pound. Higher! This time, my toes seemed to skim the mountaintop above the barrens.

It was breathtaking to go so high. Scary, but I didn't care. I'd always thought of being brave as a big thing. Fighting aliens or sailing across the ocean or singing in front of a whole church full of people all by myself. Maybe bravery didn't have to be that big, though. Today, I'd only felt a little bit braver than I was scared. Just enough to tip the scales.

But that was all I needed. I'd done brave and big-thinking things. I'd rented a booth. I'd gone to the camp by myself. I'd made a star friend, and I was swinging like I could fly. I imagined that little bit of extra brave as a beach stone, small and hard and smooth-worn. I wrapped my hand around that pretend stone to hold it tight and swung up again and again.

Until my toes touched the sky.

Chapter 9

It's always weird when I invite a friend to our apartment for the first time. Most kids don't live above a store with their grandparents.

But I had promised Salma we'd cook a test batch of blueberry enchiladas. So I brought her upstairs with me the next day. As soon as I opened the door to our kitchen, Lucky ran right over, so happy that he blocked her way, jumping and wagging.

"Let Salma come in!" I said, pulling him back.

Standing in our kitchen, Salma looked left and right,

taking everything in. "There's not much to see," I said. "But I'll give you the tour."

Her face broke into a big smile when I showed her my room. "I wish I had my own room! Even at home in Florida, I have to share a room with Emilia, my cousin who lives with us. I don't see her much, because she has a job. But her stuff is always there. You're really lucky."

Lucky's head snapped up, and Salma laughed. "No, *you're* Lucky, aren't you?"

"Living above a store can be kind of noisy," I said, so it all wouldn't seem *too* perfect. "Sometimes the lobstermen wake me up when they come into the store really early and talk to Pépère. I can hear them through the heating vent."

Salma sighed as we walked back to the kitchen. "When I want to be by myself, I have to go sit in our truck. But I have to tell someone where I'm going, because once I fell asleep out there, and my dad had the whole camp out looking for me. He thought I'd been eaten by a bear!"

I laughed. "When I first started walking to Hannah's house by myself, Mémère used to call people along the route and ask them to watch and make sure I went past. I was so mad when I found out."

I showed her Mémère and Pépère's room, the living room, the bathroom, and then we went back to the kitchen.

"Okay, what do we need?" I opened the pantry door.

Salma looked at the recipe. "The filling takes white sugar, brown sugar, cinnamon, a pinch of salt, butter, and blueberries. Then, for the tortillas, Mamá says we could buy them or make them."

"For today, let's buy them to make it easier," I said. "And we don't have any blueberries upstairs. Come on, we'll go down to the store and get some."

She grinned. "It must be great to just go downstairs anytime you need something."

"It *is* great—especially during a snowstorm. I don't even have to put my boots on!" I giggled. "I'll tell you a secret, though. We still buy some things from the supermarket in Machias when it's cheaper! But if we do that, we sneak the bags in the back door so nobody sees us."

As we came downstairs, I could see the store was busy. There were people in the aisles buying things, but my eyes skipped right over them to Mémère standing at the cash register. She was talking to Hannah.

My smile froze.

"Hannah was just asking for you. I told her you and Salma were upstairs cooking," Mémère said.

Hannah looked at Salma like she was sizing her up a little. It felt weird to have Salma and Hannah together, like I didn't know exactly who to be—the person I was with Salma or the one I was with Hannah.

"We're making a test batch of blueberry enchiladas," I said. "Salma and I decided to have a booth at the blueberry festival."

Hannah's eyebrows lifted. "*You're* having a booth at the blueberry festival?"

It felt good to surprise her, like maybe I had changed a bit, too. "Yup." I lifted my chin as I plucked a box of blueberries from the display near the register. "Are these enough, Salma?"

She nodded. "Now we just need tortillas."

"Those are in the seasonal section," I said.

Mémère and Pépère bring in a bunch of Mexican and Canadian and Central American foods every June to go with the picnic stuff, s'more fixings, and propane that mostly sell in the summertime. Mid-September, that section gets switched out with Halloween candy.

"I've never heard of blueberry enchiladas," Hannah said, following us down the aisle. "I've only ever had beef or chicken."

Hannah's usually first to do new things, so it was nice to be first for once. "They're really good." I took the blueberries and tortillas to Mémère. "Go ahead and take these out of my bee house money."

Mémère pulled the ledger out from under the counter. "Now, you three don't go making a mess of my kitchen. Be sure you clean up afterward."

Three? I touched my tongue to my top teeth. I didn't really want to be in the middle.

"I can stay awhile," Hannah said.

As we climbed the stairs back to our apartment, Salma turned to her. "I saw your picture in the festival brochure. Your dress was really pretty."

"Oh, is there a photo of me in there?" Hannah sounded innocent, but I was fairly sure she knew. "I'm always telling Lily that she should enter the pageant. It's fun, and if you win, you get a $5,000 savings bond for college. In fact, Downeast Blueberry Queen is one of the best pageants for money. Strawberry Queen at the Hillsborough Fair only gets $1,000. But since I'd already won the blueberry pageant last year, I didn't even enter the strawberry one this year."

I grinned. "If you'd won both, you'd be the Mixed Berry Queen!"

Hannah didn't seem to find that as funny as I did.

"Do you have to live here to enter?" Salma asked.

Why'd she ask that? I tried to catch Salma's eye, but she was looking at Hannah.

"No, last year there was a girl from New Hampshire in the pageant," Hannah said. "It's easy to enter. You just have to copy the form off the festival website and bring it to Mrs. LaRue at the Congregational Church. Then, the night of the pageant, you wear a fancy dress, answer some questions onstage, and do a talent."

"Oh," Salma said. "I don't have a fancy dress with me."

Whew. That solves that. Salma was pretty enough to win a pageant. But the Downeast Blueberry Queen was usually blonde, like Hannah and Mama. And white. But I couldn't say that. It would sound like we were prejudiced.

And maybe there was some of that? Or maybe the judges simply thought blondes were prettier. But either way, there was something shameful in saying that, and I didn't want Salma to think *I* thought that way.

"I'm getting a new dress for this year," Hannah said. "So I could loan you my dress from last year."

I stared at Hannah. Being Downeast Blueberry Queen was a huge deal to her. Why was she doing this? Was she trying to take Salma away from me? Or was she jealous and trying to make room for herself in the middle of our friendship? Or was she so sure that Salma didn't have a chance to win that it was safe to be kind to her?

"Tomorrow is supposed to be windy and rainy," Hannah said. "So I won't have to go fishing with my dad. If you want to, you and Lily can come over to my house to try on the dress to see if it fits."

I felt like when you're swimming and a big wave comes and just carries you along in a direction you don't want to go. A girl didn't just come into town and win the pageant. Downeast Blueberry Queen was more than having your hair done and wearing a blue dress. The winner represented our local towns—and us. The judges would never pick Salma. Plus, she wouldn't be able to do the events after the festival. She wouldn't be here.

"Would that be okay, Lily?" Salma asked. "Can we go over tomorrow?"

"Tomorrow?" I felt pulled in two directions. I thought

this was a bad idea, but Salma wanted to do it. Star friends always help each other. "Okay," I said.

Salma insisted I try the first enchilada we made. I took a bite, even though I wasn't hungry.

"So what do you think?" Salma asked. "Should we make these for our booth at the festival? Bee houses and blueberry enchiladas?"

"They're good," I said slowly. "I just have to decide if they'll sell well enough. Because that's the whole point, right? To make money for Lucky?"

"I think they'd be great," Hannah said. "They're different. A nice change from pie."

Enchiladas would be a little change to the festival, but Salma entering the pageant would be a big one. One thing I've learned from all the conversations I've overheard sitting next to the coffee station:

Some people don't like changes.

Chapter 10

Hannah's old pageant dress was blueberry blue with silvery sparkles, puff sleeves, and a huge skirt covered in swirly fabric roses. Pépère would call it razzle-bee-dazzled.

Maybe even razzle-bee-double-dazzled.

Secretly, I hoped the dress wouldn't fit. But Hannah was already in pageant mode, explaining how the whole thing worked. "The first questions the judges ask are about blueberries," she said. "Those are just facts, like

'Name the growing season for Maine's wild blueberries.' At the end of the blueberry round, the judges choose the girls who gave the best answers to go to the next round, where you do a talent and the questions are more personal. Last year, I got 'If you could meet a famous woman from history, who would it be?'"

Salma grimaced. "What if you don't know?"

"Then you smile and say the question back to the judges slowly," Hannah said.

I could tell she liked explaining it all to Salma. I'd never been much interested in the pageant.

"That gives you a few extra seconds to think about an answer. Like this—" Hannah stood up straight and took a deep breath before smiling brightly. "If I could meet a famous woman from history, who would it be? Oh, that's a hard one, because there are so *many*! But if I could meet a famous woman from history, I would love to meet Eleanor Roosevelt because she was kind and smart and brave and she did many wonderful things to make the world a better place."

"Wow," Salma said, impressed.

I nodded. Hannah was good at this, for sure. "*That's* why she's Downeast Blueberry Queen," I said.

Hannah smiled a real smile. "Last year, I also got 'What's your favorite zoo animal?'"

"Favorite *zoo animal*?" Salma asked.

"No, don't repeat the question like it doesn't make sense," Hannah said. "They'll take off points for that. If you can't think of anything, just smile and make up something that sounds like it *could* be true. As long as you're confident, no one will know the difference. Try it again. What is your favorite zoo animal?"

"What is my favorite zoo animal?" Salma said slowly. "I like elephants. They're beautiful, and, they, um, live in families and take care of one another."

"Great!" Hannah said. "See? It's not so hard. Just try not to say 'um' next time. Another question I remember was 'What do you want to be when you grow up?'"

"I want to be an artist," Salma said.

"And?" Hannah prompted. "The more you tell them, the more they'll remember you."

"I want to be an artist and live in a house that's all my own," Salma said. "I would paint my house lots of pretty colors and live there, just me and my dog, Luna."

"Great," Hannah said. "Adding in your dog is a nice touch."

Salma and I looked at each other, and I felt the secret sizzle between us. When you imagine, you can make the world be whatever way you want it to be. You can find a lost dog and keep her with you forever.

Hannah took the dress off the hanger. "Are you ready to try this on to see if it fits? The bathroom is down the hall. You can change there."

"Wow. It's heavy," Salma said, taking the dress from her.

"All pageant dresses are heavy—at least the good ones are. The crystals weigh them down."

Salma carried the dress wrapped around her arm so it wouldn't touch the floor on the way down the hallway.

Sitting on Hannah's bed, I said, "Thank you. It's nice of you to help Salma."

Hannah looked up toward the ceiling. "It kind of hurt my feelings that you left the boat landing so fast the other day. It seemed like you didn't want to be there."

"I'm sorry. I didn't mean to hurt your feelings," I said. "I just had to get back."

"Because you were doing something with Salma?" Hannah asked.

I felt my face flush, like I'd been caught in a lie. "She's

helping me make money for Lucky to have an operation on his eyes."

My friendship with Salma was much bigger than that, but Hannah might say that being star friends was silly. Or she might take it over and then it wouldn't be fun anymore. Some things are magic between two people, but they fizzle when anyone else gets involved.

I looked around Hannah's room for something else to talk about. Her room had always been as familiar as my own. On her bureau was her stuffed animal collection that we used to play with; her bookshelf was full of books I've read. We've traded books so much that it feels like we own them together.

But some things had changed. Now her bulletin board was covered with magazine photos. One was a beach with blue-green water and tall palm trees. There were glossy pictures of girls wearing clothes that no one would wear around here. And a few close-ups of boys who were probably famous, but I didn't know who they were. "Are you excited for school?" I finally asked, just to say *something*.

"Kind of," Hannah said. "I'm tired of fishing, but my dad needs me to help."

Talking to her felt uncomfortable, like talking to people I don't know very well. I was relieved when I finally heard the bathroom door open and Salma's footsteps in the hall.

The dress was so fancy that she didn't even look like herself, except for her face and ponytail and her feet in her flip-flops. "It's a little loose, but not bad," she said.

"It looks good on you." Hannah sounded surprised.

"Would it be okay if I left it here until the pageant?" Salma said. "I don't have anywhere to hang it up. And I'll have to figure out something for shoes. I have some pretty sandals at home in Florida, but I didn't think I'd need them here."

"Yeah, I don't suppose they'd work raking blueberries," Hannah said.

Was she being mean? No, Hannah looked confused. Like maybe it had been easy to offer Salma the dress when she thought Salma wasn't any real competition.

But now she wasn't so sure.

Chapter 11

Mrs. LaRue's eyebrows shot upward when Salma and I walked into her office a few days later. "Back so soon, Lily? I hope you haven't changed your mind about the booth at the festival. I'm not supposed to give refunds."

"No, Mrs. LaRue. We're dropping off an application for the pageant. This is my friend Salma."

"How nice!" Mrs. LaRue smiled, holding out her hand for the paper. "Lily, you've never entered the pageant before. Your mom would be so proud! Danielle was as pretty as a picture and had such a lovely singing voice. She still holds the record for most wins in a row."

I blushed. "No, Mrs. LaRue. I'm not entering. Just Salma."

"Oh!" Mrs. LaRue looked over the application. "Well, yes. There's no rule you have to be a resident to enter."

"I live here *now*," Salma pointed out.

"Yes, though not—"Mrs. LaRue sucked on her bottom lip, like there were words she was holding back.

I felt anger lifting up my chest. I would never want to be in the pageant, but Salma wanted to. And if a girl from New Hampshire could be in it, so could Salma! I gave Mrs. LaRue a steely look that surprised even me. "Salma's probably handled more blueberries than all the other girls combined. And we wouldn't have any blueberries for the festival if we didn't have people to rake them."

"Of course." Mrs. LaRue took a breath and turned all businesslike. "The application looks all here." She pointed at each line with her pencil to check that everything was filled in. "Name, birthdate, Social Security number for the savings bond, grade level, parents' names. Okay, I'll make you a copy of the application. I need to keep the original."

I waited while Mrs. LaRue copied the application and pulled a blue notebook from her shelf. "Salma, have you ever done a pageant before?" she asked.

"No," Salma said. "This is my first one. I thought it sounded like fun."

"Oh, it *is* fun!" Mrs. LaRue agreed. "It's the highlight of the festival! You get to dress up all pretty and lots of people come and cheer you on."

That didn't sound any fun to *me*, but Salma smiled.

"You'll be judged on beauty, blueberries, talent, and personality. The beauty portion takes into account your hair, makeup, and dress. Do you have a pageant dress to wear?"

"Lily's friend Hannah is loaning me her dress from last year," Salma said. "But I wanted to ask you about the talent part."

"Most girls sing," Mrs. LaRue said. "Dancing is also popular. One year we had a baton twirler, but that nearly ended in disaster. The baton went flying into the audience! You aren't a baton twirler, are you?"

Salma shook her head. "Could art be a talent? I could show the audience some paintings I've done."

Mrs. LaRue hesitated. "Art?"

"There's a first time for everything," I said loudly. "And Salma's art is definitely a talent."

"I guess that would work." Mrs. LaRue put Salma's application in her notebook. "Glorious Hair Styling always donates their services to the contestants at four o'clock on the day of the pageant. They'll have a space set up in a corner of the arts and crafts barn at the fairgrounds. But don't wear your pageant dress, just in case the girls at Glorious spill anything on you. The public gets to watch and sometimes those Glorious girls get chatting. Nicole Thibodeau learned that the hard way last year when one of those stylists got hair gel all over her dress's collar!"

The more Mrs. LaRue talked, the worse I felt. Salma was from the camp. She had an unusual talent. She wasn't as familiar to everyone as most of the contestants were. I'd had my doubts before, but Mrs. LaRue made them ten times worse.

"They aren't going to *cut* my hair, right?" Salma asked. "Just curl it and stuff."

Mrs. LaRue handed us Salma's copy of her application. "The stylists won't do anything you don't want them to, but if you were my daughter, I'd be right there to make sure."

I didn't think Salma's mom could come, so I said, "*I'll* make sure."

"Be at the church at six thirty. The pageant starts promptly at seven," Mrs. LaRue said.

"Do I need to bring anything other than my dress and my art?" Salma asked.

"Just a beautiful smile!" Mrs. LaRue said.

As we walked home, Salma was quiet. Then she said, "Bet they've never had a contestant from the camp before."

"No, I think you'd be the first," I said. "Are you sure you want to do this?"

"I don't know." Salma looked down at the road in front of us. "I like helping my family, but I don't want to do farm work when I'm grown-up. I don't think we'll ever have enough money for me to go to college, though. That takes *extra* money."

"Lots of extra money," I agreed.

"When Hannah said the prize was a savings bond, I thought that could be a start. And it'd be just for me—the money I make now goes to help my family. But the good thing about a savings bond is that it's for later. I'd have to keep it, like a promise for the future. Does that sound silly?"

I'd never seen Salma looking discouraged. She always seemed so sure of herself. "No," I said. "Not silly at all."

She kicked a little stone along the road. "I don't think Mrs. LaRue thought I had any chance to win, because I'm from the camp. People want us to come and work, but they want us to be invisible."

I blushed, because I knew she was right. Before Salma, I'd never given much thought to the workers and their families who came and went every summer. Mostly they kept to themselves and we kept to ourselves. They were just there, and then one day they weren't.

But when Salma became my friend, she changed that for me. She could change it for other people, too. Just like Mama being the first French Canadian girl to win the pageant had changed people's minds. I bet some people didn't think Mama had a chance, either. But she'd challenged that and showed them all.

I stood up taller. "Someone has to be first. And if any-one thinks you don't have a chance of winning, well, there's only one thing for us to do."

"What's that?" Salma asked, lifting her head.

"Prove them wrong," I said.

Chapter 12

At the beginning of summer it always feels like there's so much time ahead: whole empty calendar pages of sunshine, warm sea breezes, midnight thunderstorms, and running barefoot in the grass. Enough afternoons to do every single thing you wanted to do and even some days left over to do nothing at all.

But somehow summer fills up and flies by. Instead of feeling hopeful and free and happy as August wore on, I couldn't help feeling sad pangs that when the blueberry festival was over and summer went away, Salma would go with it.

Every chance we had, Salma and I painted bee houses. As we worked, and customers came and went from the coffee station, I quizzed her on blueberry facts.

"Okay, here's another one," I said. "Why do we still employ blueberry rakers? Why isn't the whole industry mechanized?"

"One reason is rocks," Salma said, painting tiny sea lavender flowers on her bee house. "The land is rocky, and it costs a lot of money to move boulders. People with rakes can get into places that a machine can't."

"Right." I skimmed through the *Maine Wild Blueberries* brochure Salma had picked up at the Winthrop office. "When is the wild blueberry season in Maine?"

"I'd know that one without even studying," Salma said. "Late July to early September."

"And then where will you go?" I asked.

She looked up from the flowers she was painting. "Maybe Pennsylvania for apple season. I hope so, anyway. The school I go to in Pennsylvania has the best art teacher.

Mrs. Danbury is one of my star friends. She almost makes up for fractions."

"Fractions? What do you mean?"

"My Pennsylvania school is behind my Florida school in math," she said. "Not by a lot, but they hadn't done adding and subtracting fractions when I left Pennsylvania in fourth grade, and my class in Florida was past that when I came. So I missed it and I always get adding and subtracting fraction questions wrong when you have to change the bottom numbers. I hate when people think I'm not smart or they make fun of me just because I don't know something they know."

"I don't like that, either. Does either school have after-school help?" I asked. "I had to do that with decimals. I hate the decimal point! Hard to believe something so little can cause so many problems!"

Salma shrugged. "It's too hard to stay after school because I don't have someone who can come pick me up at the right time. Give me another blueberry question."

I looked back at the brochure. "Maine harvests what percentage of lowbush wild blueberries in the USA?"

"Ninety-eight percent," Salma said.

"That's right! What's the Maine state dessert?"

"Blueberry pie," Salma said.

"Well, there was a push a few years back by the whoopie-pie people," a voice said, startling us both.

I hadn't paid any attention to Marty Johnson fixing his coffee next to us. I certainly didn't know he'd been listening.

"But the blueberry pie people won," Marty said. "How are blueberry bushes pruned?"

Salma smiled at him. "By mowing or burning. Doesn't burning kill the plants, though?"

"Only on the top. Burning keeps the weeds out and destroys disease," Marty said. "After a field is burned, the blueberries are the first plants to return. So burning gives blueberries a head start. Do you know what the top of a wild blueberry is called?"

"The calyx," Salma said. "It's in the shape of a five-pointed star."

"Atta girl!" Marty put a plastic lid on his coffee. "You keep it up! You're going to do great!"

After Mrs. LaRue's doubts, it felt really nice to have someone on our side. As Marty left, I looked back at the brochure. "When did it become popular for factories around here to start canning wild Maine blueberries?"

"During the Civil War. Cans of blueberries were sent to feed the Union Army."

At my feet, Lucky startled and gave a little bark. I looked down the store aisle to see that a lady had come in with a German shepherd. The dog was wearing a red-and-black service dog vest.

"Shh. It's okay, Lucky," I said. "He's just visiting. He won't hurt you."

Lucky was on his feet now, tail wagging. I had to grab his collar to keep him from going down the aisle to the dog.

"Lucky wants to make a friend," Salma said.

"You aren't supposed to distract service dogs," I said. "And Lucky gets so excited. It might annoy that dog. Or he might worry Lucky would hurt his person." Gripping him by the collar, I looked back at the brochure. "How do wild blueberries make new plants?"

"They spread underground by rhizomes," Salma said, "which create new roots and stems. A wild field has lots of different rhizomes all running along under the ground, so that's why there can be so many different blueberry colors, sizes and, um?" She made a face.

"What's the matter?" I asked.

"I'm trying so hard not to 'um'! There can be different colors, sizes, and—?"

"Flavors," I said, setting Lucky back under the table. "We can stop now if you want to. You already know more about blueberries than I do!"

"But I have to be one of the best," Salma said. "Or I won't get to show my talent."

The chime above the door sounded as the woman with the service dog left the store. Good!

Lucky lay back under the table and rested his chin on my foot. I waited a few seconds to be sure he would stay, then I picked up a new bee house and the autumn leaf stencil. I hadn't done that one in a while.

"Why don't you try doing a bee house without the stencil?" Salma asked. "It might look better than you think."

"It might look worse, too."

She shrugged. "But at least it would be yours. That's what I like about art. It lets me become more like myself, not more like everyone else."

Well, that was all well and good for *Salma*. I would never have signed my bee houses or called them "art," but it still stung to hear her say the stenciled bee houses weren't even mine. "Not everyone's as good at painting as you are, and I want these to sell," I said sharply. "It doesn't feel like the right time to try something new."

"Maybe you're scared to try?" Salma asked.

"Like you're scared of fractions?" My eyebrows came down. "I can't afford to waste these houses."

"So what about the blueberry enchiladas?" Salma asked. "Are you going to take a chance on them?"

"Yes." I had already decided that we could give away little samples, and then people could try them if they weren't sure about buying a whole one.

She smiled. "Mama said she'd be glad to make us the tortillas. But I can't bring the blueberries. Mr. Winthrop lets us pick a few to eat ourselves, but I couldn't pick them to sell."

"I know where I can pick some," I said. "You don't have to help me, though. You have to do that all day long."

Salma shrugged. "It won't feel like work if we do it together. I can bring a couple of rakes so it'll go faster. Where should I meet you?"

"It's not far from your camp. I'll walk over and get you tomorrow night after supper." As I taped the autumn leaves stencil on my bee house, I glanced down to the brochure open on the table. "When was the first blueberry rake invented?"

"1910."

I kept asking, and she kept answering until the drying shelf above my table was full of bee houses.

Chapter 13

The next day, I ate supper early so Salma and I could pick blueberries for a long time before it got dark.

I walked Lucky over to the camp. This time I didn't stop at the office. Mr. Winthrop hadn't made me sign in last time, and I wasn't sure how he'd feel about visitors bringing dogs.

Some kids were playing tag around the cabins, and a woman was hanging out clothes on a rope tied between two trees. Lucky let me go first. He was sniffing right and left—there were new smells to check out. "Come on," I said, pulling him along.

Salma's mother was sitting on the sill of the doorway, painting her toenails with gold nail polish. "Stinks!" she said, pointing to her foot.

I nodded. "I like the color, though."

"Hi, Lily!" Salma came through the doorway, nudging past her mom, making the tiny brush spread gold over her mom's toes, messing them up. "Salma!" she scolded.

"Sorry, Mama. I'm borrowing two blueberry rakes, okay?" She grinned at us. "Hey, Lucky!"

His tail started wagging like crazy. He pulled forward on his leash, trying to find her. Salma sat down on the grass and Lucky climbed right into her lap—which was funny because he's so big that Salma couldn't even see over him.

"Lily, here." Mrs. Santiago motioned me to sit next to her.

Salma said something impatiently in Spanish and her mom said something back, but finally her mom shook her head and Salma's shoulders slumped. "She wants to paint your fingernails. I told her we're in a hurry, but she said it dries fast."

I don't paint my fingernails very often, and I've never had them painted gold. But if Salma couldn't talk her mom out of it, I didn't stand a chance.

I gave Lucky's leash to Salma and sat down.

Mrs. Santiago took my hand and started painting. I'd never sat next to Salma's mom before. The only mom I'm used to sitting next to is Hannah's mom, so this felt tingly—weird and nice and sad, all mixed together.

"Are you sure you don't mind helping me pick blueberries?" I asked Salma. "'Cause it would be okay if you didn't want to."

"I don't mind." She peeked around Lucky and grinned at me. "I bet I'm faster than you!"

I laughed. "I'm sure you are!"

As the tiny brush moved over my fingernails, my hand didn't even look like mine. When my ten fingers all ended in gold, Mrs. Santiago held my hands and blew on them.

I swallowed hard, sorry we were done. "Thank you— gracias. They look pretty."

"Come on," Salma said. "I'll grab the rakes. Your nails can finish drying on the way."

I looped Lucky's leash around my arm so I could hold my hands out and wouldn't risk smearing the polish. As we walked, I glanced back a couple of times to Mrs. Santiago sitting in the doorway. It was such a little thing to put polish on someone's fingernails, but it was a mom thing, and it made me all messed up inside to have someone treat me like a daughter.

The only place I could see my own mom was where Salma and I were heading. When we got to my blueberry-picking spot, Salma dropped her blueberry rakes and made the sign of the cross: forehead to heart, shoulder to shoulder. "A *cemetery?*"

"I always pick here, because these blueberries don't belong to anyone in particular. They're everyone's blueberries."

Lucky waited patiently while I opened the metal gate. "It's fenced in, so I can let him run free in here." I clanked the gate closed behind us.

"Won't he get hurt running into the gravestones?" Salma asked.

I smiled, unclipping his leash. "Watch him."

Lucky sniffed the air and then took off running down the lanes of the small cemetery, turning each corner perfectly.

"How does he know?" Salma asked.

"He'd been here lots of times when he could see." I threaded the limp leash through the fence so it'd be ready for our walk back home. "Things don't change here, at least not very often. So he remembers where everything is." I watched him sniff the pathway between two stones. Yellow-and-black butterflies and mason bees flittered around him. When he could see, he used to snap at bugs that flew by. Now they have to be close enough for him to hear them.

Along the chain-link fence, the berries were so thick that the bushes looked blue from this distance. "The blueberries are best over there," I said, pointing. "They don't mow too close to the fence so the bushes grow bigger."

Our feet crunched the reindeer moss under our feet, as loud as if we were walking through autumn leaves. The only other sounds were the wind blowing the little American flags on the soldiers' graves, the buzz of insects, the chirp of birds, and the occasional rumble of a car driving down the gravel road that ran past the cemetery.

"Do you worry about ghosts?" Salma asked. "I knew someone who was followed home from a cemetery by a ghost. At least that's what she said."

I looked at the gravestones, all facing the blueberry barrens across the road, like they were watching over them. "That would be okay with me if it were the right ghost."

"Is your mom here?" Salma asked.

I nodded and led her past the rusted metal trash barrel and some gravestones with faded fake flowers and little solar lights, all the way to the pink granite stone with the bear cub on top. When she was small, Pépère called Mama his little bear. It's weird to think of my grown mom being someone's little girl.

"What happened to her?" Salma said.

The breeze blew a strand of hair across my nose. I let it stay there. "She was in a car accident." I didn't look at Salma, because saying that always stops a conversation cold. The other person never knows what to say, and it makes me feel doubly bad. Bad for the truth and bad for making *them* feel bad. "She and Mémère got in a fight over something Lucky did. So she left. She was driving on a back road and she hit a moose. They're dark brown, so they don't show up at night very well, and she must not have seen it, because there weren't any skid marks on the road to show that she tried to stop."

Everyone says it was over instantly. I hope that's true. I hope it happened so fast that she and the moose didn't have even one second to be scared.

"It's too bad she didn't stay in Florida," Salma said. "We don't have moose there."

"Yeah, but after Florida she went to New York. That's where she met my dad. So if she had stayed in Florida, I wouldn't be here," I said. "I don't remember her, though. I was only two when it happened."

And that feels like the biggest cheat. I had her every day for two years, but I don't remember. I wonder sometimes, if time travel were real and I could magically go back and meet her when she was my age, would we like each other? I've always been scared that I'd like her, but she wouldn't like me back. She'd think I was boring.

Salma put her arm through mine. "Mama says people can feel it when you think of them. It's like a warm feeling that suddenly comes over them," she said. "So I think of Luna every day."

I don't know if that's true, but being with Salma made me want to believe it. I imagined Mama as hard as I could: my big-thinker, blueberry queen Mama, packing Lucky and me in her car to come home to Mémère and Pépère.

Could Mama feel that warm feeling? Was she somewhere in Heaven above the stars, knowing she was in my heart?

"Maybe you should plant tiger lilies here," Salma said.

"I don't think the cemetery association lets you plant things. They need to be able to mow," I explained. "Plus, lilies grow wild along the roadsides here. They're weeds."

"Only because somebody said so," Salma said. "Lilies are proud and sassy. They don't know they're weeds." She gave me a huge grin. "And the cemetery association couldn't keep weeds out, right? Weeds grow where they want."

I imagined a patch of tiger lilies under the ground all winter and blooming every summer for Mama. A burst of orange among the blue, green, pink, and gray.

The sun was getting lower over the trees on the far side of the barrens. Salma went to work near the fence. With one hand she held her rake and the other swung free, her gold nails flashing in the sunlight. I wondered if she'd painted them herself or if her mom had done hers, too.

I picked up the extra rake and joined her. Most times when I gathered berries I picked them one at a time with my fingers. The rake felt heavy as I pushed the tines into bushes near the ground and pulled up and back through the tiny branches. "Raking is so much faster than picking." I tipped the rake so the berries would roll down and collect near the handle.

"Much faster," Salma said. "But my arms and shoulders feel it every night. Ever since you showed me the star on the top of the blueberries, I imagine that I'm gathering stars, not blueberries. Bins and bins full of stars."

Holding the rake above my bucket, I watched the leaves blow off sideways in the breeze as the blueberries rolled down, plinking into the bucket. "Did you ever read that picture book, *Blueberries for Sal*? It's from a long time ago. Sal is a little girl and her mom takes her blueberry picking."

"No. Is her name Salma?"

"Maybe," I said. "I don't think it says—just Little Sal. Anyway, Pépère used to read me the story. I still have the book."

It was Mama's book. Sometimes I opened it just to see her name written inside. "Little Sal and her mom go blueberry picking on a hill, and Sal keeps eating berries," I explained as we raked. "Her mom walks too far ahead and she thinks Sal is still behind her. But Sal has slowed down because she's eating blueberries. Also, there's a mother bear and her cub, Little Bear, eating berries on the same hill. Neither mom knows the other is there. Sal ends up wandering over near Little Bear's mother and Little Bear goes over near Sal's mother. Both moms think it's their own baby behind them until they turn around."

"Then what happens?" Salma asked.

"They both get a big surprise! Then they get their own kid back."

I wish that book were real, except for the bear parts. I wish Mama could just turn around and realize she'd gone too far ahead without me. Then she'd come back to find me.

"Is that all?" Salma asked. "That's the whole story?"

All? "Well, yeah. It's a happy ending. Everyone was back where they belonged."

"It's only a happy ending if you *like* where you belong," Salma said. "Do you always want to live here?"

"Maybe when I'm grown up I'll live somewhere else," I said. "But Mémère and Pépère are here. I'd want to be able to see them and come here to visit Mama. So I don't think I'd move too far away."

"I wish I felt like that," Salma said. "One of the worst parts of moving around is that the only place I feel like I really belong is in our car. I like the idea that if I won the pageant, it would matter that I'd been here. I wouldn't just be another kid who came to rake blueberries and then everyone forgot."

"I won't forget you. And neither will Lucky." A pin-prick of guilt poked at me because Salma was helping me make money for Lucky's surgery, and she had reasons she needed money, too. But Lucky's surgery cost so much. There wouldn't be any extra that I could give her. It hurts to want two things, but know that you can't have them both. But I couldn't give up on Lucky. He needed me.

"You can visit me and Luna when I get my little house someday," Salma said. "You can bring Lucky with you."

I nodded, but I knew the truth. Lucky was already old. He wouldn't be with me when I was a grown-up. And neither would Luna. Dogs don't last that long.

But we were just pretending, and Salma said that when you pretend, the world can be any way you want it to be. "When I come, I'll bring Lucky and some blueberries to make blueberry enchiladas," I said.

"And I'll wear my crown from the pageant!"

The sun was low in the sky by the time we'd filled our big bucket with berries. Lucky waited patiently at the gate as I clipped his leash back onto his collar.

"You can tell your pépère that you picked blueberries with Sal!" Salma said. "And Lucky is our bear."

"And we have a bucket full of stars."

"Minus one," Salma said, popping a blueberry into her mouth. "Now the star is inside me."

She handed me a tiny blue-black berry. "Wish before you eat it."

My first-choice wish would be to go back in time and fix things that had already gone wrong. But not even wishes can do that.

I couldn't choose between Lucky and Salma, so I picked a second berry, a rosy-pink one. *One wish for Lucky.*

One wish for Salma. So they could both have what they wanted.

I put the blue-black berry in my mouth and bit down. A warm blue explosion, tasting of earth and sunshine. *Let me raise enough money to fix Lucky's eyes.* Then, on the rosy pink one, I wished, *Let Salma win Downeast Blueberry Queen and get that savings bond.*

Walking home, we ate more warm berries, until our teeth were full of seeds and our lips and fingers were blue. Red berries and blue berries. Black ones and purple ones, and even a few that were striped. Sweet and tart and in between.

Filling us with stars.

Chapter 14

The day before the pageant, I took out my copy of our to-do list:

1. Cook the blueberry filling for the enchiladas. (Lily)

2. Make tortillas. (Salma)

3. Choose three bee houses to show off for the talent part of the pageant and practice what to say about them. (Salma)

4. Pick up Salma's dress at Hannah's and let Salma borrow my white sandals. (Lily)

5. Finish painting the last few bee houses so they'll dry in time for the festival. (Lily)

6. Pack up everything for the festival. (Lily)

7. Ask Pépèrè to drive Salma to the arts and crafts barn by 4:00 for hair styling. (Lily)

8. Be at the church at 6:30 for the pageant. (Salma)

9. Cross fingers. (Both)

Making the blueberry filling ahead would save us time. Then I could just heat it up on festival day. As I cooked, the whole house smelled bluelicious, like it does when Mémère and I bake pies. When I was done, I set the huge pot of filling to cool on top of the microwave (the only place I was sure Lucky couldn't reach it), and turned off the stove.

"Stay," I told Lucky as I headed for the door. But he whimpered and wrinkled his brow. "Okay, come on."

Lucky jumped around the kitchen with so much joy that I had trouble clipping his leash on.

It would be smarter to leave him home, because the next thing on my to-do list was get Salma's dress. I wasn't sure how I would hold Lucky's leash and carry that heavy dress. But I'd just have to figure it out when I got there.

As I led Lucky down the stairs, I saw Pépère talking to Miguel. Mémère was over at the cash register ringing up a blueberry pie for a family of tourists. "I'll be back in half an hour," I called to her. "I have to pick up Salma's dress for the pageant."

"We have schedules for the Downeast Blueberry Festival in a pile under the bulletin board," Mémère said sweetly to the family. Then she looked at me. "Call if you're going to stay awhile. Be safe."

Mémère can carry on several conversations, even in different tones, all at the same time. "Why are you taking that dog with you?" she asked. "He'll get that dress all dirty."

"He's not going to *wear* it," I said.

Wrong thing to say. Mémère's look was scalding. "Pageant dresses are looked at very carefully by the judges. What if Lucky steps on it or makes you fall down carrying it? You can't just throw a dress like that in the washing machine!"

I huffed. *How would she know?*

Sometimes understanding comes in little drops, and other times it rushes in like the tide, rolling everything over as it comes. Mémère must've helped Mama in the pageant.

Had they gone shopping for a dress together?

Did she help her get ready?

Maybe that's why Mémère always took care of the store on festival days. I assumed it was because *someone* had to. But maybe it was just too hard?

My chest felt heavy with words I wished I could say and questions I longed to ask, but Mémère was telling the tourists to have a nice day.

As Lucky led the way outside, I wondered if Mémère had been proud of Mama winning the pageant? Mama must've answered her questions really well to win three years in a row. I wish I knew what they'd asked her. Even more, I wish I knew her answers.

It hurts not knowing the big things, but it also aches not knowing the little ones. What was her favorite zoo animal? What famous person did she wish she could meet? It wouldn't even matter what her answers were, I'd just like to know.

When I saw Dr. Katz in her garden, I pulled Lucky's leash back.

"Hello!" Dr. Katz called. "What a gorgeous day for a walk."

"Yes, I'm heading over to Hannah's to pick up a dress for the blueberry pageant."

Dr. Katz put down her trowel and stood. "Are you in the pageant?" she asked, dusting the dirt off her jeans.

"No, my friend Salma is in the pageant, and Hannah's loaning her a dress. I'm going over to get it," I said. "But I'll have a booth at the festival! I'm selling bee houses and blueberry enchiladas."

"Wow! That's wonderful." Dr. Katz came across her yard toward us. "I'm glad you're selling your bee houses. I haven't had a chance to come to the store to buy some, but I'll be at the festival. I'm volunteering at the Humane Society's booth giving free rabies shots. I'll stop by your booth when I get a chance." She reached her hand out so Lucky could sniff her. "Let me look at those eyes."

I waited, my heart beating hard, while she examined Lucky. "How do they look?" I clenched my teeth, bracing myself in case it was bad news.

"No worse, but no better. Really about the same."

Whew! There was still time to save him. "I'm hoping to make lots of money at the blueberry festival for his operation."

She opened her mouth, but I held up my hand. "I know! It might not work. But as Pépère says, 'You never know what you can do until you try.' Right?"

She nodded. "Yes. But please just remember that it's a lot to put an old dog through surgery."

"Being blind is a lot to put him through, too," I said firmly. "And this is his big chance. I'm going to do everything I can for him."

Dr. Katz smiled. "You're strong-willed like your mother, Tigerlily."

Strong-willed? I didn't think of myself that way, but Dr. Katz seemed sure. "Do you know that you're the only person I let call me Tigerlily?" I told her. "Because you make it sound like it's a good thing."

"It *is* a good thing," Dr. Katz said. "Tiger lilies are beautiful flowers, and it's a beautiful name. Your mom chose it. I think she'd like to hear it."

I wanted to see my name as beautiful, like Mama and Dr. Katz saw it. A flower, not a weed. "With most people, it's easier to be Lily," I said. "But *you* can keep calling me Tigerlily."

She nodded. "I'll see you at the festival, Tigerlily."

Stopping to see Dr. Katz meant I was a little late getting to Hannah's. But that was okay. I could just grab the dress and get back quickly. I still had things to do.

I expected her mom to answer the door, but Hannah herself did. "Hey! I thought you'd be fishing!" I said.

"We came in early so Mom could do the final fitting for my pageant dress."

Lucky jumped around Hannah's kitchen, so happy to be with her that he knocked a magazine off the table with his wagging tail.

"I have Salma's dress ready." Hannah took a garment bag down from the pegs in the kitchen. I was relieved to see the blue sparkly dress was zipped up safely. It couldn't get dirty and it'd be easier to carry.

"Do you want to see *my* dress? Mom was just steaming it," Hannah said. "This year I wanted to stand out by wearing a different color."

A sparkly silver dress with a blue sash hung next to the refrigerator. "Wow. It's so shimmery," I said. "Like a fish."

Her smile dropped.

"A *pretty* fish. Like a trout in the sun." Wrong thing to say. This was not going well. "Or like sun sparkles on the ocean!" I added quickly.

"I just hope I made the right choice to go with silver." Hannah ran her tongue over her bottom lip. "Winning last year means people expect more from me this year."

I wondered if Mama worried about that, too. Did each year feel harder than the year before? How'd she keep going for three years in a row?

"So are you cheering for me tomorrow night?" Hannah asked. "Or for Salma?"

I was surprised to see worry in Hannah's eyes. At first I didn't know how to answer it. Both of my friends wanted to win.

But then it surprised me how clearly the answer came. "Salma needs to win more," I said.

Hannah looked away from me. "Okay. I'll see you then."

Walking home, Lucky pulled on his leash, wanting to hurry. I had so much left to do, but I couldn't make my feet go faster. Hannah and I had been two peas in a pod for a long time, but she had left that pod first.

Now I had, too.

_____

That night, I sat down at my painting table and picked up the last two blank bee houses. I stenciled maple leaves in autumn colors on the first one. Then I picked up the blueberries and bees stencil.

And I paused.

I wanted these houses to sell. This didn't seem like a good time to try something new. I still didn't want to waste a bee house with an artistic mistake.

But I put down the stencil anyway.

The front of the bee house wasn't any bigger than usual, but somehow it felt huge. I didn't even know what color to start with.

Salma wouldn't worry about that. She'd just pick up any color and begin. So I chose orange. I painted six wide, long petals, fanning out from the center like a sunburst. I added a spattering of tiny black dots.

Staring at it I saw something that I'd never noticed before. Those orange petals made a six-pointed star. On a flower that grows where it wants. A flower that doesn't know it's a weed.

I painted more orange star flowers, covering the whole front of the bee house. It wasn't perfect or neat. Not one tiny bit ordinary. Then I picked up my littlest brush and painted my name in teeny letters down at the bottom.

TIGERLILY.

Chapter 15

For most of the year, the fairgrounds looked like a ghost town, boarded up and forlorn, but for a few glorious days every late August the boards came down and the whole place burst into life.

Pépère and I loaded up our truck with a table and signs and Salma's pageant dress and sandals and the three bee houses she'd picked to show for her talent. Then we set off for the camp to pick her up.

As the truck bounced along the road through the barrens, my heart beat so hard I wondered if Pépère could hear it. "Did you ever get nervous when Mama was in the pageant?" I asked him.

He smiled weakly. "Like a long-tailed cat in a room full of rocking chairs. She always did well, but it's hard to be in the audience. You want to help, but at that point, there's nothing you can do but hope."

"But by the *third* time she entered, you must not have been nervous. Right?"

He shook his head. "It didn't matter. I always wanted her to get what she wanted. It didn't matter how many times. She wanted to win and I wanted it for her."

"Why'd she want to win so bad?" I asked.

"She always liked to prove a point," he said. "In her day, the kids who were from French Canadian families didn't mix much with the other kids. But she was smart as a whip and pretty as a picture. And when Danielle wanted something, there was no talking her out of it." He sighed. "Not that I ever tried. When you love someone, you want what they want. She wanted to show everyone that French Canadian girls were as good as anybody else."

"It's hard to imagine anyone felt that way about French Canadians."

Pépère nodded. "Times change. And it's good that they do. But it only happens if someone is brave enough to be first."

"Like Salma," I said. "I wish I was brave like that."

Pépère grinned. "Well, I'll tell you a secret. I had to give Danielle a pep talk every year on the church steps. She'd suddenly get so nervous that she'd want me to take her home and forget the whole thing."

"Mama? Really?" I'd only seen the photos of Mama after she'd won. "What was she scared of?"

"That people wouldn't think she belonged up there with the other girls. Or that she'd embarrass herself and forget the words to her song. Or she'd trip on her dress."

I stared straight out the side window of the truck and let the blueberry barrens turn into a green-blue blur. I had never imagined Mama scared about anything.

Salma was waiting for us at the entrance to the camp. "Ready?" Pépère asked as she hopped into the truck beside me. "Let's go get you gussied up."

Pépère and I quizzed her on blueberry facts all the way to the arts and crafts barn at the fairgrounds. We couldn't stump her, though. Salma knew every answer.

Once we arrived, everyone got quiet. One end of the arts and crafts barn was in the process of being set up with the prize-winning quilts and flower arrangements and baskets and other things that people had made. The far end of the barn looked like a beauty parlor. Some pageant contestants were already wearing black plastic capes and sitting in the folding chairs with hair stylists behind them. Hannah was there, the front of her blonde hair up in clips, while her hairdresser curled the back. I was glad that Hannah was busy talking. I wouldn't have known what to say after "Hi."

There was a weird combination of smells: old barn wood and hair spray. In the background were banners announcing the pageant and posters advertising hair products. On the opposite barn wall was a double line of eight-by-ten-inch framed photos, starting with black-and-white and ending in color—every Downeast Blueberry Queen since the first one in 1942. Right in the middle of the line was Mama smiling back at us three times.

I'd seen these photos before, but I looked again, searching deep into her eyes. I hadn't ever noticed, but along with the happiness on her face, I saw relief. I felt closer to her knowing she'd been scared.

"I'll pick you girls up here in an hour or so and take you to the church," Pépère said, beside me. He turned and strode up the long center aisle back toward daylight, like it was too hard to be there another minute.

Each hairdresser from Glorious Hair Styling had been assigned one potential blueberry queen. Salma's girl had "Brittany" on her name tag.

As Salma climbed into the chair, a surprised look passed between Brittany and Marcy, the stylist next to her. Brittany had dark hair, but with lighter stripes in it, kind of like a skunk. I found a folding chair so I could sit close enough to stop her from doing that to Salma.

"Could you sit up straighter?" Brittany asked Salma. "And where do you live, honey?"

"Mostly Florida," Salma said, "but my family is working at Winthrop Blueberries for a little while longer."

"Oh, are you staying in one of those cute, little blue houses?" Brittany asked brightly. "I've always thought that would be fun. Like camping."

"It's not camping. It's work," I snapped.

But Brittany chatted on. "I like to camp in the mountains. We pitch a tent and cook outside." She picked up a lock of Salma's hair and studied it. "You have beautiful thick hair. But you have some split ends at the bottom. Can I trim them? It'll give your hair more bounce."

"How *much* are you cutting?" I asked. Salma's mom wasn't there to make sure Brittany didn't go wild with Salma's hair, so I'd do it.

Brittany's thin, little eyebrows went up, like she was just noticing I was there. She pinched Salma's hair between her index and middle finger and showed about two inches. "Right here."

"That's a lot," I said.

"If it'll make my hair better, it's okay," Salma said.

Brittany looked smug, like we'd been fighting and she won. "What does your dress look like, honey?" She clip-clip-clipped, hair falling to the floor.

"It's blue and silver," Salma said. "Hannah loaned it to me. She wore it last year."

I glanced back to Hannah still talking to her stylist. I couldn't hear the words, but her tone carried—extra cheerful, already in pageant mode.

"Oh, I remember that dress!" Brittany said. "Hannah is such a nice girl. I did her hair last year, and she won! We did side ringlets and a bun for her. That wouldn't look right on you, though. Your hair is too thick for that. I could give you an updo, but I'm thinking your hair would look really pretty in a side-swept style."

I fidgeted until Brittany finally put down her scissors and picked up her comb. She moved the part in Salma's hair a bit to the right, and then brushed Salma's hair all over to the left. She held it in a side ponytail. "We'll give you a pony that ends in a mass of curls. Or we could do a braid if you'd like. What do you think?"

"Curls," Salma said.

I had to admit Salma's hair was looking very pretty, though it didn't really look like Salma. Then again, Pageant Hannah didn't really look like Regular Hannah, either.

"Close your eyes, sweetie," Brittany said when she finished curling.

Salma coughed at the cloud of hair spray.

"You look fabulous!" Brittany unhooked Salma's plastic cape. "Now, when it's time to get dressed, be sure that you step into your dress. Don't pull it down over your head or you're going to mess up all my hard work. Here's a mirror so you can have a look."

Salma held up the hand mirror and her whole face changed. A huge smile lit up her eyes. I was so happy that she liked how her hair looked.

"Mama!" Salma said, hopping out of the chair.

Mrs. Santiago was coming up behind us. Salma ran to her and hugged her. Holding up her ponytail, Salma showed her mom her curls.

"What does this cost?" Mrs. Santiago opened her purse.

"Nothing," Brittany said. "We donate our services to the pageant. But a pair of dangly earrings would really complete Salma's look." She showed off her own earrings and then pointed to the items for sale. "We sell some over on the product wall if she doesn't have any."

"It's okay, Mama," Salma said. "I don't need earrings."

But Mrs. Santiago was walking to the display of shampoos and nail polishes and sparkly jewelry and bows. She came back with a pair of rhinestone dangly earrings that glittered. "These are good?" she asked, handing them to Brittany.

Salma hugged her mom's side. "They're perfect!"

Mrs. Santiago put her arm around Salma and spoke softly to her in Spanish. I didn't know the words, but I could tell from her tone that it was a mom thing. I looked down at my flip-flops, wishing Pépère was there to get me.

"Lily, here."

I looked up to see Mrs. Santiago holding her other arm open to me. My feet ran without me even telling them to. Holding me, she rested her cheek on my hair and said something tender in Spanish.

It was a mom thing.

Chapter 16

As we walked through the front door of First Parish Congregational Church, Mrs. Santiago carried the pageant dress, still in its garment bag, over her arm and the white sandals in her hand. Beside her, Salma held her three bee houses.

"Rosa, we'll save you a seat," Pépère said to Salma's mom. "Come on, Lily. The good seats go fast."

Part of me wanted to go with Salma and her mom, but there probably wasn't enough room in the ladies' room for all three of us.

"Good luck, Salma!" I held up my hand and crossed my fingers. "We'll be cheering for you."

She held up one hand and crossed her fingers, too.

The closest Pépère and I could get to the front was the third row of pews. Hannah's mom and dad were in the front row. Last year, I would've gone over to say hi, but it felt too awkward now. I wasn't sure what Hannah had told them or what kind of reaction they'd give me. *If they turn around, I'll go over,* I decided, but they were busy talking to some people I didn't know. One of them was a boy.

Was that the Amazing Brandon? The hair color looked right, but I couldn't be sure. I'd only seen a few photos and never one of the back of his head.

My feet bounced, until Pépère reached over and put his hand on my knee. "You're shaking the whole row," he whispered.

"I can't help it!" Waiting for something you want is so hard. I wished the pageant were already done, and Salma had won, and I had earned enough for Lucky. Everyone would be happy.

But after the festival, blueberry season would be just about over. And then Salma would go. I didn't like to think about that.

I tried to stop fidgeting, but that just made it worse. Like trying not to scratch a bug bite. By the time the church was nearly full and Salma's mom had joined us, I felt like I would burst from waiting.

"Is Salma okay?" I asked her.

Mrs. Santiago nodded. "She is ready."

Music started and I turned to look back toward the door. A line of girls was coming down the aisle, like a bunch of blue sequined bridesmaids at a wedding.

In the back row of pews sat a group of workers from the camp. I hadn't thought about how they might show up to encourage Salma—but she was part of a whole community there. Salma's dad was smiling. He was dressed up in an embroidered red shirt with buttons. Not a T-shirt like he usually wore.

I couldn't help feeling a pinprick of jealousy that Salma's dad and mom were both there. It didn't feel fair to envy Salma, but it was a big thing to have your parents come to watch you do something new and important. There were lots of things I would've traded to have it, too.

There were ten girls, all in blue, except one girl in purple and Hannah in silver. Hannah's stylist at Glorious

Hair had created lots of ringlets that bobbed as she walked.

But Salma stood out, too. Her dark hair and brown skin drew your eye right to her. "She looks beautiful," I whispered to her mom.

As they reached the stage, each contestant took a seat in the line of folding chairs. I let go a deep breath to see that Salma was in the middle. Probably the best place to be, I thought. Not first. She'd have the chance to watch some others before her. But not last, either, where she'd have the most time to feel nervous, waiting through everyone else.

Mrs. LaRue walked up to the pulpit. She was dressed in a long blue dress and a glitzy necklace and high heels. She pulled the mic down closer to her mouth. "Good evening, ladies and gentlemen! Welcome to this year's Downeast Blueberry Queen Pageant! Let's begin by standing and singing 'America, the Beautiful.'"

The church filled with creaky-board sounds as people stood up from the pews. The organ played a few bars of getting-ready music, and we sang.

O beautiful for spacious skies,
For amber waves of grain,

For purple mountain majesties
Above the fruited plain!

I wondered if "fruited plain" included blueberry barrens. Or if the migrant workers from Honduras and Mexico knew those words.

I turned to peek. A few workers were nodding their heads to the music, but most just stood there, wide-eyed, like they didn't really know what to make of all these sequins and sparkles in church. Or that big lady at the pulpit singing heartily off-key.

America! America!
God shed His grace on thee,
And crown thy good with brotherhood
From sea to shining sea!

Mrs. LaRue belted that song out like an opera singer on public TV. I wondered how all this sounded to Salma and her parents. Crazy, probably.

"Now I *know* you will recognize our master of ceremonies!" Mrs. LaRue said.

Bob Kiddle, the TV weatherman from Channel 5, came to the mic, followed by a peppering of applause. "Thank you. It's going to be a wonderful pageant and a great start to the Downeast Blueberry Festival," he said. "But first, I'd like to introduce a few people. Your judges tonight are Lorraine LaRue, Jack Winthrop of Winthrop Blueberries, and Sheriff Mark Cotton. We also have some visiting dignitaries. Let's give a big Downeast welcome to the Strawberry Queen and her court from the Hillsborough Fair! Girls— or should I say 'Your Majesties'? Please come up onstage!"

Three girls, wearing crowns and red dresses, came forward: two about my age, and a little one. The Strawberry Queen and Princesses smiled and waved, then sat in a line of chairs beside the judges.

"And Miss Maine Sea Goddess and Sea Princess from the Lobster Festival."

Up came two more girls wearing crowns and waving, except they had rhinestone starfish in their crowns.

Beside me, Mrs. Santiago ran her fingers along the strap of her purse, over and over.

"Some past Downeast Blueberry Queens are in the audience! Ladies, please stand up and be recognized!"

Clap, clap, clappity-clap. I looked around to see various women stand up. If Mama had been here, would she have been proud, like these women? Or embarrassed? Maybe she would've given a funny royal wave to the crowd and a wink to me.

I wondered if Pépère was thinking of her, too. I reached over and put my fingers over his.

He gave them a squeeze.

Bob Kiddle said, "Now, it's time to get down to business. The Downeast Blueberry Queen! This year, we have a beautiful set of young ladies. Let's get to know them." He picked up a page of notes. "Step forward and tell the audience where you're from when I call your name."

The first girls just said a town. "Machias." "Addison." "Milbridge." But when it was Salma's turn, she stepped forward with her hands clasped in front of her and said in a clear voice, "Florida."

Bob Kiddle chuckled. "Well, now! You're a long way from home, Salma!"

He teased the other contestants, too. "You're blinding me with those sequins, Hannah!" "Josie, you are certainly a Monroe with that red hair!" but somehow that didn't seem hurtful. Mémère might've said I was being too sensitive, but I thought Mr. Kiddle was not being sensitive enough by pointing out that Salma wasn't from here.

"The contestants are scored for beauty, knowledge of blueberries, talent, and personality," Bob Kiddle explained to the audience. "All those scores will be added together, and the highest score will be our new Downeast Blueberry Queen and the winner of the $5,000 savings bond. The runner-up, Blueberry Princess, will receive a one-hundred-dollar festival gift certificate, and all the contestants get a coupon to use at Glorious Hair Styling. Are you ready, ladies?"

The girls onstage nodded, curls and earrings bobbing.

Beside me, Salma's mom was now clutching her purse. "She'll do well," I whispered to her. "She knows the answers."

She nodded.

"First up is the blueberry round. That will determine which girls go on. Amber, we'll start with you," Mr. Kiddle said. "What percentage of lowbush wild blueberries in the USA is harvested in Maine?"

Darn! Salma would've gotten it right for sure.

"Ninety-eight percent."

"Very good, Amber!" Bob Kiddle said. "Carly, tell me a health benefit of wild blueberries."

"Wild blueberries are a rich source of antioxidants!" Carly said.

"Hannah, when is the wild blueberry season in Maine?"

She smiled and leaned into the mic so everyone could hear. "The wild blueberry season is late July to early September."

"Excellent!" Bob Kiddle said. "Salma, what special name did some of the early Wabanakis have for blueberries?"

Salma grinned and looked right at me. "Star berries, because there's a five-pointed star on the top of each one."

I grinned back, my whole inside collapsing with relief.

As the questions came and went, I thought the answers in my head when Salma's turn came up. Just in case ESP worked and she could read my mind.

"When was the first blueberry rake invented?"

1910. 1910. 1910.

"1910," Salma said.

It was hard to keep track of all the questions and who gave the best answers, but Salma only missed one.

"Salma, what famous poem was written by Robert Frost about our state fruit?" Bob Kiddle had asked.

Uh-oh. She glanced at me, but I didn't know, either. That wasn't in the brochures. I shrugged, palms up.

"Blueberries for Sal?" she asked.

"No, sorry. *Blueberries for Sal* was a children's book, written by Robert McCloskey. 'Blueberries' is a poem by Robert Frost."

But other contestants had gotten some answers wrong, too. Mindy Gaudet forgot half the ingredients of a blueberry pie, and Amy Osgood said blueberries were canned during the Revolutionary War.

"Well done, everyone!" Mr. Kiddle finally said. "Have the judges picked the top contestants to go on to the next round?"

Mrs. LaRue brought him a folded white card.

"The three contestants moving on, in no particular order, are—" Mr. Kiddle opened the card.

He paused so long that I wanted to run up onstage and snatch the envelope out of his hand to read it myself.

"Amber."

"Hannah."

Mrs. Santiago grabbed my hand. I clenched my teeth together as hard as I could. *Please, please, please.*

"And Salma!"

If I hadn't been in a church, I would've jumped up and screamed. But one look at Salma and I knew something was wrong.

Even from the third row, I could see her hands were shaking.

Chapter 17

As Bob Kiddle set up a standing microphone for Amber to sing "Amazing Grace," Salma had her hands clasped tightly in front of her.

Amber didn't seem to think "Amazing Grace" was enough on its own, so she added a lot of up and down notes to jazz it up. I looked to see how the judges were taking it. Mrs. LaRue was smiling, but her eyes weren't pleased. Mr. Winthrop looked amused, and Sheriff Cotton was reading his notes.

"Some things don't need bee-dazzling," Pépère whispered to me.

"Thank you, Amber! That was very moving and quite spirited!" Bob Kiddle said. "And now Salma has something to show us! We'll give her a minute to get ready."

Salma turned and left the stage. I took a deep breath. My legs bounced, all my worries and nervousness bobbing with them.

Except Salma didn't come right back.

Any second now, I kept thinking as the seconds piled up. *Now.*

"So, um, let's go on to Hannah's song," Bob Kiddle finally said. "And we'll come back to Salma. While Hannah is setting up, let me tell you about some of the wonderful events at the festival tomorrow."

My heart clenched. Salma wouldn't *leave*, would she?

"I'll go check on her," I whispered to Mrs. Santiago. Being in the middle of the row, I had to climb past a whole bunch of knees to get out. "Excuse me. Excuse me."

Hannah was singing "Over the Rainbow." I hoped she was so busy singing that she didn't see me sneaking out the side door.

I opened every door in the hallway until I found the right one. Salma was sitting on a chair, holding her bee houses on her lap.

"What's the matter?" I asked, kneeling beside her.

"I don't think this is a real talent," she said.

"Of course it's a real talent! Do you think 'Amazing Grace' sung like you're on a roller coaster is a real talent?"

But Salma didn't look convinced. She held out one hand so I could see it tremble. "My hands are shaking. At first, I thought the pageant would just be fun. Then I really wanted that savings bond. But I'm not like Hannah. I wasn't born here, and this isn't the right kind of talent to win. So why am I doing this? The judges would never vote for me. I'm just going to look silly."

I couldn't believe how scared she seemed to be. And I suddenly realized that this was about more than winning a savings bond for her—it was about showing she mattered. That she belonged and had a place here, even if she couldn't stay.

I stood up. "Remember that day we were swinging at camp? I was feeling a bit scared, and I realized something. To do brave things, you don't have to be hugely brave. You only have to be a little bit braver than you are scared. Give me your hand."

Salma held out her hand. I put my fist on her palm and opened my fingers. "I pretended that little bit more brave was a rock. Here it is."

Salma wrapped her fingers around as if she were holding it.

"You said people want migrant workers to be invisible," I said. "Show them that you aren't. I'll be your assistant, just like those ladies on TV game shows. I'll hold up your bee houses and show them off. All you have to do is tell about them. Okay?"

I could hear applause and Bob Kiddle's muffled voice congratulating Hannah.

And to my relief, Salma stood up.

Bob Kiddle looked quite surprised to see me. As I walked across the stage holding Salma's bee houses, my head suddenly woke up to what was happening. My heart had been so intent on helping that I hadn't thought about the fact I'd be onstage in front of the whole audience. My mouth went dry.

I wasn't dressed for this in my jeans and T-shirt and sneakers. Passing the line of chairs, I couldn't even look at Hannah.

I stood in the middle of the stage next to Salma and placed two of the bee houses on the floor. I held up the other one—covered with multicolored bees. I turned it, first to face the judges, then to the audience on the right, in the middle, and on the left.

"My friend, Lily, sells these bee houses for mason bees. This summer I've been helping her paint them," Salma said quietly, her hand fisted, like she was holding my pretend stone. "What I love about art is that anything is possible. Bees can be pink. Trees can be purple. It's like taking the world as it is and then swirling it around to show how it could be." Her voice grew stronger as she spoke.

I looked down at Pépère grinning at me. Mrs. Santiago was wiping her eyes. In the row behind Pépère, Brittany was proudly elbowing another hairdresser from Glorious, like it was her big moment, too.

My gaze strayed to Hannah's mom and dad, and I gave them a tentative smile. They smiled back, though they looked a bit confused. The boy with them wasn't paying attention at all. He had his head down, looking at his phone.

The second bee house was covered in Salma's exuberant flowers. As I showed it off, Marty Johnson caught my eye and gave me a thumbs-up. Dr. Katz waved to me. Salma's dad and the people from the camp were standing up at their seats in the back to see better. Everyone was smiling or looking thoughtful as Salma talked.

"I think art can take ordinary things and show them to you like it's the first time you've ever seen them," she continued. "And you realize that even ordinary things aren't really ordinary at all."

Maybe that's true, I thought. Maybe when we see things all the time, we stop really looking at them. And it takes an artist, someone who can look past the ordinariness, to remind us how special they really are.

I reached down and traded the second bee house for the last one. This one had all different sizes and colors of blueberries—each with a yellow star.

"Not everyone likes things that are different," Salma said, sliding me a tiny smile. "In fact, when I first got to Maine, I received a pork pie as a present."

The audience laughed.

"I didn't think I'd like it. But Lily gave it to me, and she said it was famous. So I took a chance on it. In fact, my whole family did. And it was good!" Salma stood up straighter, looking right out at the audience. "It's scary to try something different when you don't know how it'll work out, but that's when the best things can happen. The things that surprise you and change you. Those things can make *you* different."

There was a long pause and then the clapping started in the back row and surged forward, like a wave rolling up the beach, carrying along everyone as it came.

I reached down and picked up the bee houses, sure now that everything would be all right. Salma had finished the hardest part of the pageant. She had done really well.

Answering a few personal questions was the only thing left. All she had to do was tell the truth. This would be easy.

I should've known, though.

Real truth is never easy.

Chapter 18

Back in my pew in the audience, I felt weak with relief as Bob Kiddle brought out a fishbowl filled with small folded pieces of paper. "Let's find out a little more about our three finalists: Amber, Hannah, and Salma. Ladies, as I call your name, please walk over here and choose a question. Amber, you're first."

Amber came forward, smiling at the audience. She picked a little folded paper from the fishbowl and handed it to Mr. Kiddle.

"Amber, what is your favorite childhood memory?" he read.

"My favorite childhood memory is the time my family went to Disney World when I was eight," Amber said. "I loved going on the rides. And we went in February, so we flew away from all the ice and snow in Maine. I changed from my snow boots into my sandals on the plane."

"We can all relate to that!" Mr. Kiddle said.

I bristled. The migrant workers weren't here in February. They couldn't relate to it, and they filled up the whole back row.

Hannah walked up to take a question from the fishbowl. Even though she was beaming, I knew she was worried. I wished Hannah didn't have to lose for Salma to win.

"How did you feel meeting the other contestants?" Bob Kiddle asked Hannah.

She kept smiling, but I could tell she was trying to figure out the best way to answer that. "Meeting the other contestants was fun! I knew some of the girls from school, but it was nice to meet the others, including Salma. We met over the summer. She borrowed a dress from me."

Did she *have* to say that? I wondered if Hannah was trying to win by showing off her kindness. Loaning Salma her dress *was* kind, but it also showed everyone that Salma didn't have what she did.

Salma came forward to choose her question. I pointed at my mouth. *Smile.*

"What is your favorite subject in school?" Mr. Kiddle asked.

Salma finally smiled. "Art!"

Everyone laughed, because that was no surprise after seeing her bee houses.

"I like art because there are no wrong answers," Salma said. "It's all about how you see the world. So you can be completely yourself."

Around me, the audience gave a soft appreciative *hmm.* It was a nice sound, a soft hum of approval.

Pépère leaned across to whisper to me and Mrs. Santiago. "She's bee-dazzling!"

As Amber and Hannah took their next turns, I watched the girls who didn't make it past the blueberry round, still sitting in the chairs behind Mr. Kiddle. They were smiling, but every now and then the smile was replaced with a big sigh or a look of boredom. And the littlest Strawberry Princess was pulling a string on the hem of her red dress.

Bob Kiddle unfolded Salma's next question. "What's something you're still learning or working on?"

Salma rolled her eyes. "Fractions!"

The audience laughed loudly. I looked at the judges and was glad to see they thought it was funny, too. Salma was killing this, and she was doing it by being honest.

I hoped Bob Kiddle would say that was the end of the questions, but they kept coming. "Amber, if you win, whom will you thank?"

"My parents, the judges, and the whole community!" Amber motioned with her hands to the audience, like she was an orchestra conductor.

"Describe your best friend," Bob Kiddle asked Hannah.

She looked first toward her parents and the boy sitting with them, then I saw her gaze slide away and right to me. For a second Hannah's smile slipped and she looked sad. "My best friend is Lily. We've been friends since we were little."

My eyes locked with hers.

"Lily's pépère always called us 'two peas in a pod,'"

she said, not even blinking. "We've both gotten busy and I haven't seen her as much. I miss her."

"It's good to have a true friend!" Bob Kiddle said.

I watched Hannah as she walked back to her place in line. She didn't look at me again, though. Maybe she just said the first thing that came to her mind. Or maybe she thought I'd be a better answer than the Amazing Brandon.

Or maybe she missed how things used to be, too.

"Salma, tell us something you've learned this summer," Bob Kiddle said.

"I've learned lots of things this summer—especially about blueberries!" she said, and the crowd laughed. "But I've also been learning about blind dogs."

Bob Kiddle took a tiny step backward. "Blind dogs?"

Salma nodded. "My friend's dog is blind, and I wanted to know everything that could be done to help him. I had to do that research really early in the morning, though, because that's the only time I could get a turn on the camp computer."

"Did you find out anything interesting?" Bob Kiddle asked.

"Yes. I did," she said.

I wanted to yell, "What?" but Bob Kiddle was moving

on. "Now for the final questions. This is your last chance to impress the judges, ladies!"

She'd gotten up early to learn about Lucky? She'd done that without even telling me.

Beside me, Pépère blew out a loud breath. He'd been nervous for Salma, too. I grinned at him and he held up one finger.

One more question.

My legs couldn't help bouncing again as Amber and Hannah answered their last questions. Finally, Bob Kiddle unfolded Salma's. "Tell me something you'll never do."

Her smile fell, just like her lips were on a string and someone tugged it down.

Oh no, I thought. You don't have to take it so seriously. *I would never lie.*

I would never cheat on a test.

I would never wear a plaid skirt with striped socks.

She answered so softly that if she hadn't been right up to the mic, I don't think anyone would've heard her. "I'll never stay in one place," she said, and she walked back to her spot in line.

When the winner was called, it was Hannah.

Chapter 19

The next day was a picture-perfect, sunny day with a bright blue sky and fat white clouds. Before the festival opened, I set out our signs explaining what we were selling and how much they cost. I arranged all the bee houses at one end of our booth. I put my tiger lily house toward the back because it wasn't anywhere near as good as Salma's. But it was still nice to see it there.

At the other end, Pépère stirred the blueberry filling in a large Crock-Pot next to napkins, paper bowls, plastic spoons, and a can of whipped cream for anyone who bought a blueberry enchilada.

A few minutes before nine o'clock, Salma came by the booth, dressed in her pageant dress, carrying two bags of tortillas. "Mama made these this morning so they'd be extra fresh," she told me. "I wish I could stay with you, but I'm supposed to help Hannah with the pie-eating contest."

On his mat beside me, Lucky lifted his head and wagged his tail. If he could've seen Salma, Lucky might not have recognized her all dressed up in her pageant dress and runner-up crown and sparkly earrings, her hair in a side ponytail still curly from last night. But that's one thing about being blind. What you look like doesn't matter to Lucky. He sees you with his heart.

"Don't you worry, Blueberry Princess," Pépère said. "I'm here to help Lily. She'll sell the bee houses and I'll serve up those blueberry crepes."

"They're *enchiladas*," I said impatiently. "Be sure you say that."

"Oh, right," Pépère said. "They're a first cousin to crepes, though."

"I'll be back when the pie-eating contest's done," Salma said. "Mama's bringing me some regular clothes so I can change afterward. I hope you sell lots of bee houses and enchiladas before I get back."

"Thanks!" I said. "Good luck with the pies."

She headed toward the pie-eating contest platform, holding up her dress so the bottom wouldn't touch the grass.

My heart felt like someone had punched it. We'd both pinned a lot of hope on her winning. Maybe the judges wanted someone who lived here to win so she could visit the nursing homes and attend the parades after the festival. Or maybe Hannah just got better scores. Maybe singing is an easier talent to judge than art.

Or maybe Salma's last answer was too honest, too hard to hear. But whatever the reasons, somehow the pageant didn't seem as big a deal to me as it always had. It showed part of our community, but not the whole thing.

"Lily?"

I looked up to see Hannah standing in front of our booth, all glitzy in her silver pageant dress, wearing her huge crown. "I just wanted to say hi and that I hope you earn all the money you need for Lucky," she said.

I swallowed hard. "Thanks. And congratulations."

"Thank you," she said. "You know what I said last night about you being my best friend? I feel like we've gotten sidetracked or something, but I really meant it."

"I miss you," I started, but there was something else I had to say. "But lately you only want to talk about the Amaz—um, Brandon."

"I'm sorry." She sighed. "Brandon came last night and then he spent the whole pageant playing games on his phone! He's nice, but not my type."

A giggle exploded inside me. *Not your type? Since when? Five minutes ago?* But I choked that giggle back down. Hannah was asking to try again, and I wanted that more than I wanted to be a smart aleck.

"Maybe we could do something tomorrow?" Hannah asked. "You, me, and Salma? I haven't been swimming much this summer. We could show Salma how cold the ocean is in Maine."

"Okay," I said. "But let's go all the way down to the point to go swimming. I want to make sure Salma sees at least one lighthouse before she leaves."

"Great!" Hannah smiled. "That'll be fun." Watching her walk away, holding her crown with one hand so it wouldn't tip off her head, I wasn't sure if we'd ever be the same kind of friends we'd been when we were little. Maybe being two peas in a pod was over, but maybe we could be more like two wild blueberries: two of a kind, but different, too.

When Sheriff Cotton cut the blue ribbon that stretched from one traffic cone to another across the festival entrance, a surge of tourists and locals rushed in. Old people with cameras, parents with strollers, kids with dogs. There were people everywhere.

Lucky stayed on his mat, but his nose kept sniffing. A little Pomeranian on a leash was so small that he could see under the booth. He yapped at Lucky.

Lucky wiggled his way forward, but he was tied to the table and couldn't reach him. "We don't know if that dog's friendly," I said, pulling Lucky back.

Marty Johnson was the first person at our booth. "I came here as soon as I could. I want that pretty bee house Salma showed at the pageant last night. The one with the colorful bees. I figured I'd better grab it before someone else does."

Earlier in the summer, I might've felt jealous that Marty wanted Salma's bee house and not mine. Now I was just happy to imagine her bee house in Marty's yard, a little piece of her that was staying here.

"Marty, would you like to try a bite of blueberry enchilada?" Pépère asked. "We have samples on the plate here."

"Those do smell delicious," Marty said. "I've never had one of these, but I'll try a bite."

Dr. Katz was right behind Marty. "Tigerlily, I see you have a couple helpers!" She smiled at Pépère and Lucky. "Lucky is such a good boy to stay so patiently right here."

Lucky's head turned at his name and his tail wagged.

"That's because I keep giving him bites of crepe— enchiladas," Pépère said.

"He's excited about the other dogs," I told her. "But I can't risk him getting hurt or running off and getting lost in all these people. I thought he should come, though. He's the whole reason I'm doing this."

Dr. Katz nodded. "I need to get to the Humane Society booth. But first, I came to buy some bee houses for my garden. I'd like two, and my eye goes right to those glorious flower ones."

I picked up two of Salma's best bee houses.

"Actually, I do want this one with the little purple

flowers," Dr. Katz said. "But I also want the one in the back. With the tiger lilies."

I stared at where she was pointing. "But *I* did that one."

"Then I'll love it even more," she said, smiling.

Maybe she just bought it to be nice, but I didn't care. I was so happy imagining Salma's and my bee houses together in Dr. Katz's garden.

We had a crowd in no time. I sold lots of bee houses. I hoped the people who bought Salma's would take good care of them.

Pépère could barely keep up with the blueberry enchilada samples. Most people who tried a bite bought a whole one.

"Wow! I've never had one of these before," Mrs. LaRue said, licking the last bits of blueberry enchilada off her spoon. "It's quite delicious."

When she smiled, I had to stifle a giggle because her teeth were blue!

"These are houses for mason bees," I explained to a tourist wearing a MAINE sweatshirt. "You put one near your garden and it encourages the bees to stick around and pollinate your flowers and plants."

She chose the bee house that Salma had painted with multicolored blueberries and yellow stars.

"Here's our artist coming right now!" Pépère said.

Salma was wearing shorts and a T-shirt, carrying her crown under her arm, though her hair and earrings were still pageant fancy.

"You were wonderful last night," Mrs. LaRue said. "The competition was very close, you know."

Salma gave a little smile, but I knew it wasn't a real one. I think "almost" is one of the hardest kinds of losing. Because you could see all the way to winning before that door shut.

"How was the pie contest?" I asked.

She rolled her eyes. "A kid got a blueberry up his nose, and one of the adults lost her contact lens in the pie."

"Eww," I said.

"The whole time, I was worried I'd get blueberry stuff on Hannah's dress. I was relieved to finally give it back to her." Then Salma smiled—a real one. She handed me a white envelope. "I have something for you, Lily."

I opened it, and it was a festival gift certificate for one hundred dollars.

"As Blueberry Princess, I won this gift certificate. I

can use it at any booth at the festival, so I'm using mine for Lucky."

"Thank you!" I counted in my head. We had several hundred dollars in the cash box last time I added it all up—now a hundred dollars more—and it was still early! But when I looked closer, I saw the gift certificate had been written out to the Machias Humane Society. "Wait. What?"

"When I read about blind dogs, it said maybe what would help Lucky the most was another dog," Salma said tenderly. "Dogs are pack animals, so another dog could lead him and be Lucky's eyes for him. I was going to talk to you about it, but then I got this gift certificate and it seemed like fate. So I just did it."

I was confused. "You want me to get another dog to lead Lucky around? But that's not the plan. I want him to see for himself."

"I know, but when I read about it, it said the operation doesn't always help," Salma said. "And it's risky because Lucky's old. It said there was a chance that maybe he wouldn't make it, and—"

"It would've been better if you had spent the gift certificate here," I said. "At *this* booth."

"I thought this would be better for Lucky, and he'd even like it more."

Better for Lucky? "He's *my* dog," I said, annoyed.

Salma crossed her arms over her chest. "It was *my* gift certificate."

How could she suggest that I wasn't thinking of Lucky when I'd been thinking of him my whole life? I thrust the gift certificate at her. "Then *you* get a dog!"

Salma stood there with her mouth open.

"I didn't mean—" I started, but she turned and pushed her way through the crowd.

Tears came to my eyes, right there in front a family of tourists who came over to buy blueberry enchiladas. I couldn't believe I'd said that—it had just flown out of my mouth. She'd lost her dog and couldn't have another, and I'd just shoved that at her with the gift certificate. But why didn't she understand? All this time we'd been working on making Lucky see again. I couldn't just give up on him!

As Pépère squirted the whipped cream on the family's enchiladas, he said, "Lily, do you remember how I said that when you love someone, you want what they want?"

"Exactly!" I said. "I want Lucky to see again. Salma knew that."

"Yes, *you* want Lucky to see. But what does Lucky want?"

I looked at Lucky, his head still pointed in the direction Salma had gone. His tail wagged a few times hopefully. "He wants to see."

"I don't know about that," Pépère said. "He already seems very happy to me. That's something we could learn from dogs, isn't it? They don't keep looking backward at what they've lost or asking 'why me?' They just move on and find a new way to be happy again."

As the family walked away with their enchiladas, Pépère said, "It wouldn't hurt to talk to the people at the Humane Society booth, would it?"

"Yes, it would," I said. "It would mean giving up."

"No," Pépère said firmly. "Giving up and letting go are two very different things, Lily. Giving up is admitting you're beat and walking away. Letting go means you're setting something free. You're releasing something that's been keeping you stuck. That takes faith and more than a little courage."

I touched Lucky's head and his tail immediately started wagging. "Mémère would never say yes to us getting another dog," I said.

"Well, there's one way to find out," Pépère said. "I'll call her and tell her to meet us here."

"She won't leave the store on such a busy day," I said.

"Oh, she'll come!" He winked. "If I tell her we're thinking of getting a second dog, she'll be here lickety-split!"

Another dog? That wasn't the plan. Lucky would like a friend, and it could be fun to have two dogs, but—

"Mémère doesn't even like *Lucky*," I said.

"We outnumber her." Pépère picked up the gift certificate and the cash box. "So what do you say? Are we going over to talk to the Humane Society people or not?"

"Okay, but I just want to talk to them. I'm not ready to decide." I turned over one of my signs and wrote, BEE BACK SOON.

Chapter 20

At the far end of the booths at the Downeast Blueberry Festival, the Machias Humane Society was selling leashes and collars, treats for dogs and cats, and T-shirts for people that said, WHO RESCUED WHOM? Behind the table, a man and a woman wearing those T-shirts were chatting with customers. And off to the side, Dr. Katz was sitting at a table, talking to a couple as she gave their big white dog a shot.

Part of me hoped there wouldn't be any dogs to adopt.

Then my decision would be easy. I could just go back to my original plan.

But I knew there were dogs, even before I saw them. Lucky's ears perked up and he tilted his head, curious. Next to the booth were two animal pens. One pen had a litter of adorable mixed-colored kittens climbing over one another. All those little green eyes and tiny tails. Some kittens were meowing. Others had their paws up on the pen, trying to get out.

Lucky sniffed that pen, but then he pulled to go to the other one. Inside were two small dogs: one brown and fuzzy and one with a smooth yellow coat. The little yellow dog came over to the side of the pen and sniffed, nose-to-nose with Lucky, tail wagging.

That yellow dog was so cute and funny, I couldn't help smiling. She had small triangle ears, and her black nose seemed too big for her face. She dropped to a play position with her front feet down and her back end high in the air, tail wagging.

But Lucky couldn't see her asking to play.

"Making a friend, Rosie?" the woman at the booth asked.

"Lily here is wondering if maybe there is a good match for her dog, Lucky, who is blind," Pépère said. "We've heard that sometimes another dog can help one that's blind and give him a better life."

The woman from the Humane Society smiled. "It looks like Lucky has chosen his own match," she said.

I looked back to see Lucky in the play position, too. The pen was still between them, but he knew the little dog wanted to be friends, even though he couldn't see her.

"Rosie is a sweetheart. She's two years old and very friendly," the Humane Society lady said. "We don't really know what kind she is, a mix of some sort. We've only had her with us for a couple of weeks. Her owner was an elderly lady who went into an assisted living home where she couldn't take Rosie with her."

Rosie seemed like a nice dog, and Lucky did like her. But it's so hard to change your mind once you've set your heart on something. "I just want everything to be the way it used to be."

"I know," Pépère said. "But maybe another dog could give Lucky something he's *never* had. What do you think, Lily?"

From behind us came a voice, "I think that one dog is problem enough!"

Uh-oh.

Mémère, mad as a wet blue jay, strode up to Pépère. "Armand! What are you thinking? Have you forgotten what it's *like* to bring a new dog home? When Danielle brought Lucky, it was a long time before he behaved! And you're just like her! Rushing into things! If she hadn't brought that dog home—"

"Lucky was a puppy. None of it was his fault," Pépère said. "When he's gone—"

"When he's gone, no one will be getting into the trash!" Mémère finished for him. "Or have to be walked or—"

"It will kill me when Lucky's gone!" The words burst out of me so hard, they hurt my chest. Lucky left Rosie and came to me with his tail down, sure my outburst was his fault. I stroked his ears until he raised his head. I looked right into his clouded eyes. "I'm sorry, Lucky. It's not your fault, not one little bit. You're the best thing I have left of her."

His tail wagged. He was always ready to forgive me when I was sorry.

When I looked up, I was surprised to see tears in Mémère's eyes.

Pépère put his arm around her. I expected Mémère to pull away, but she leaned into him. "You've got to let some things go, Marie," he said. "Danielle would want her dog to be happy. But more than that, she'd want her *girl* to be happy."

Mémère sighed so deep that she seemed to deflate right in front of me. She took off her glasses and wiped her eyes. It felt like such a personal, private thing to see Mémère, who was always sure of everything, look so lost. "It's hard for me to let things go," she said. "Because sometimes when you let them go, they're gone for good. You don't get them back."

I felt awful that I'd made her cry. "I love you, Mémère," I said softly.

She was so quiet that I didn't know if she'd even heard me, but when she looked over at me, I saw tenderness in her eyes. "I love you, too. You mean more to me than I can ever tell you, Lily. You are the heart of my heart."

I ran to her and she held me tighter and longer than I could ever remember her hugging me before. Then she sniffed loudly as she put her glasses back on. "You'll do everything for that dog, except for when you're in school."

Was she saying yes? It sure sounded like it, so I nodded. "Okay."

Mémère shook her head at Pépère. "I hope you're happy, Armand. Now I'll have *two* dogs driving me crazy."

As Pépère signed the adoption paperwork, Lucky licked Rosie's nose through the bars of her pen. And I knew right then that there are worse things than being blind. Being alone was worse. Having regret was worse. Losing someone you loved was worse.

"Pépère, when we get home, I need your help with something," I said.

He smiled as I told him my plan. "That's a great idea."

I searched all over the fairgrounds for Salma, but I couldn't find her anywhere. So on the way home, we took Rosie to the camp. Pépère stayed in the truck with Lucky, because I didn't want to overwhelm Salma's family with two dogs in that little cabin. I didn't even know if Salma would want to talk to me. "Come on, Rosie," I said.

Mrs. Santiago answered my knock.

"I need to tell Salma something," I said. "Please?"

She moved aside and I saw Salma sitting on her bunk.

"I'm really sorry," I said. "You knew how to make Lucky happy."

Rosie pulled to go meet Salma. I dropped her leash and she hopped up on Salma's bunk. It's pretty near impossible to stay mad when a dog is licking your face.

And your arm.

And then your neck.

Salma gave a small smile and then a big one. "I hoped you'd pick this one."

"Lucky picked her. Her name is Rosie and she knows it, so I'm going to keep it. But I did give her some middle names. Her full name is Rosie Luna Salma Santiago Dumont."

Salma kissed Rosie Luna Salma Santiago Dumont's head. "I like it." Then she reached under her cot and pulled out her Blueberry Princess crown.

"PRINCESS Rosie Luna Salma Santiago Dumont!" she said, placing the crown on Rosie's head.

Dogs always forgive you when they know you're sorry.

And so do star friends.

Chapter 21

After the blueberry barrens are raked, they turn rusty red until fall when they're burned or mowed to start their rebirth. The raked berries are frozen or canned or dried, and then shipped all over the world to end up in muffins and pancakes and other things. I wonder if people who open those packages and jars ever think about where those berries came from, how far away from home they've traveled, and all the hands they've passed through to bring them to their table. And would they be surprised to know that some of those hands were kid-size?

I guess some people would care, and some people wouldn't. But as Pépère says, "It takes all kinds of people to make a world."

Each year when Mr. Winthrop calls the end to the blueberry harvest, it's celebrated with a soccer game on the barrens. The rakers divide into teams based on where the players are from. Whichever team won last year's Blueberry Cup gets a free pass to the finals. Last year, Honduras won, so the United States was playing Mexico this year for the semifinals.

"Canada tried to get a team together, but they didn't have enough people who wanted to play," Salma told me as I settled Lucky and Rosie onto the blanket that we'd spread out to sit on while we watched the game. I looped their leashes around my ankles and then crossed my legs, so they couldn't go anywhere.

"I'm so glad Rosie and Lucky are getting along." Salma scratched both their bellies, one with each hand.

"Dr. Katz says Lucky is getting so good at following Rosie that from a distance, no one would even know that he's blind."

At first it had been a little hard on me that Lucky had taken to Rosie so well. Of course I wanted it to happen, but I couldn't help a pang of missing that I used to be the one Lucky depended on. But I'm learning it's okay to let Rosie do things for him, too.

I even caught Mémère slipping Rosie and Lucky some bacon one morning when she was cooking breakfast and didn't know I was watching. When I thanked her, she said, "It fell on the floor."

But then she smiled. We both knew different.

"I've brought you something," I told Salma, reaching for my backpack.

Salma stopped scratching, and Lucky pawed the air to find her hand to keep it going.

"I took all the money that you and I had earned painting bee houses, and Pépère bought you a savings bond with it." I held out the envelope to her.

She didn't take it. "You didn't have to do that."

"We earned it together." I put the envelope in her lap. "School costs a lot more than this, but it's a start."

Salma ran her fingers over the envelope.

"You need an account, so Pépère set it up. We got your Social Security number off our copy of the pageant application, and inside the envelope is a certificate that has all the information on it." I opened my backpack again. "I brought you something else, too. It's not as fun as the first thing, though." I pulled out a little notebook and a pencil. "In between soccer games and whenever this game gets boring, I'm going to teach you how to add and subtract fractions."

Salma rolled her eyes. "Do we have to?"

"Yup," I said. "If you want to go to college, you can't be afraid of fractions." I flipped open my notebook, before Salma could think of any excuses not to do this. "They're only hard until someone shows you."

As Lucky and Rosie napped in the sun, the United States and Mexico battled it out on the soccer field. And Salma practiced making the denominators the same.

As the game wore on, I made the problems harder. "Why is it so complicated?" she asked, irritated. "It seems harder than it should be."

I shrugged. "That's math for you. But the good part is that once you learn it, it doesn't change. You always do it the same way."

By the time the Hondurans took the field to warm up,

Salma was doing the problems on her own. "This really isn't as hard as I thought it was," she said.

I nodded. "I'm going to tear out these notebook pages for you to take with you, okay? Then if you forget, you can look back at these examples and remember."

"Thank you. I have something for you, too," Salma said, putting down the pencil. "It's big, though. Stay here. I'll go get it."

Waiting for her, I watched the soccer ball zipping down the field. It didn't seem one hundred percent fair that the Blueberry Cup winner from last year only had to play one game, especially when the other teams were tired out from playing one another, but I guess that's life. It's not always fair, but you have to show up and play your best anyway.

Salma came back, carrying a big piece of paper in front of her. I could tell there was something on the other side, but she held it against her so I couldn't see. "Mr. Winthrop liked my bee houses at the pageant so much that he asked me if I'd paint him a few pictures for the Winthrop offices. He bought me some paints and paper and he even paid me. I painted two pictures of the barrens for him, and I painted one for you, too." She turned the paper around. "So you won't forget me."

It was a painting of three dogs, one black, one yellow, and one bright white, running under a night sky full of stars, across the barrens dotted with blueberries. And along the edge of a far-off road, a patch of tiger lilies.

"This winter, when I look up at the stars, I'll imagine you in Maine playing in the snow with Lucky and Rosie," Salma said.

"And I'll imagine you in Florida wearing shorts and flip-flops and painting beautiful pictures." Reaching for it, I also imagined Luna running right off the edge of the painting and up the steps of Salma's house. Home again after a long time away.

And Mama looking down from Heaven, smiling to see those tiger lilies.

Then I saw something in the painting I hadn't seen at first. All around the dogs—under their paws, along the little road, even surrounding the tiger lilies—the blueberries were different colors. Red, pink, purple, black, blue, white, and even some with stripes.

On each little blueberry was a tiny dot of yellow.

A whole galaxy of stars.

Find Humor and Heart in the Novels of Cynthia Lord

A Newbery Honor Book

When Lucy enters a photography contest, she works with Nate, the boy next door, to find the perfect subjects for her photos…but in the process, she really learns to see herself.

To save the only school on their island, Tess's parents open their home to a foster child who changes all of their lives.

Catherine's life revolves around her autistic brother, and the rules that help him cope, but when her life turns upside down, she has to learn some new rules of her own.

SCHOLASTIC
scholastic.com

Available in print and eBook editions.

CLORD